ARTHUR SYMONS (1865 – 1945), was a British poet, critic and magazine editor. A leader of the symbolists in England, he interpreted French decadent poetry to the English through translations, criticism, and his own imitative poems. His important works include *The Symbolist Movement in Literature; The Romantic Movement in English Poetry*; and studies of Baudelaire, Blake, and Rossetti.

William Blake (1757 – 1827) was an English painter, poet and printmaker. He is considered a seminal figure in the history of the poetry and visual arts of the Romantic Age. His prophetic poetry has been said to form "what is in proportion to its merits the least read body of poetry in the English language". His visual artistry led one contemporary art critic to proclaim him "far and away the greatest artist Britain has ever produced". In 2002, Blake was placed at number 38 in the BBC's poll of the 100 Greatest Britons. He produced a diverse and symbolically rich oeuvre, which embraced the imagination as "the body of God"or "human existence itself".

Hundreds of books have been written on Blake, to understand and evaluate his skills, vision and views, some of which were enigmatic to many, but none more impressive and lasting than Symon's. Besides narrating the early childhood and youth of Blake along with interesting incidents, the book describes his creativity in the fields of painting, poetry, political views and enlightenment philosophy. His life in London and Felpham with its preoccupations has been ably captured. Some letters which give a glimpse of the events of that time have been included and make an interesting reading. Stanzas from Blake's famous poems have also been given which enrich the text.

WILLIAM BLAKE

ARTHUR SYMONS

ATLANTIC
PUBLISHERS & DISTRIBUTORS (P) LTD

Published by
ATLANTIC
PUBLISHERS & DISTRIBUTORS (P) LTD
7/22, Ansari Road, Darya Ganj, New Delhi-110002
Phones : +91-11-40775252, 23273880, 23275880, 23280451
Fax : +91-11-23285873
Web : www.atlanticbooks.com
E-mail : orders@atlanticbooks.com

Branch Office
5, Nallathambi Street, Wallajah Road, Chennai-600002
Phones : +91-44-64611085, 32413319
E-mail : chennai@atlanticbooks.com

First Published 1827

Printed in India at Nice Printing Press, A-33/3A, Site-IV, Industrial Area, Sahibabad, Ghaziabad, U.P.

To

AUGUSTE RODIN

Whose Work is the
Marriage of
Heaven and Hell

INTRODUCTION

I

When Blake spoke the first word of the nineteenth century there was no one to hear it, and now that his message, the message of emancipation from reality through the 'shaping spirit of imagination,' has penetrated the world, and is slowly remaking it, few are conscious of the first utterer, in modern times, of the message with which all are familiar. Thought to-day, wherever it is most individual, owes either force or direction to Nietzsche, and thus we see, on our topmost towers, the Philistine armed and winged, and without the love or fear of God or man in his heart, doing battle in Nietzsche's name against the ideas of Nietzsche. No one can think and escape Nietzsche; but Nietzsche has come after Blake, and will pass before Blake passes.

The Marriage of Heaven and Hell anticipates Nietzsche in his most significant paradoxes, and before his time, exalts energy above reason, and Evil, 'the active springing from energy' above Good, 'the passive that obeys reason.' Did not Blake astonish Crabb Robinson by declaring that 'there was nothing in good and evil, the virtues and vices'; that 'vices in the natural world were the highest sublimities in the spiritual world'? 'Man must become better and wickeder,' says Nietzsche in *Zara-thustra*; and, elsewhere: 'Every man must find his own virtue.' Sin, to Blake, is negation, is nothing; 'everything is good in God's eyes'; it is the eating of the tree of the knowledge of good and evil that has brought sin into the world: education, that is, by which we are taught to distinguish between things that do not differ. When Nietzsche says, 'Let us rid the world of the notion of sin, and banish with it the idea of punishment,' he expresses one of Blake's central doctrines, and he realizes the corollary, which, however, he does not add. 'The Christian's soul,' he says, 'which has freed itself from sin is in most cases ruined by the hatred against sin.

Look at the faces of great Christians. They are the faces of great haters.' Blake sums up all Christianity as forgiveness of sin:

> 'Mutual forgiveness of each vice,
> Such are the gates of Paradise.'

The doctrine of the Atonement was to him a 'horrible doctrine,' because it seemed to make God a hard creditor, from whom pity could be bought for a price. 'Doth Jehovah forgive a debt only on condition that it shall be paid? ... That debt is not forgiven!' he says in *Jerusalem*. To Nietzsche, far as he goes on the same road, pity is 'a weakness, which increases the world's suffering'; but to Blake, in the spirit of the French proverb, forgiveness is understanding. 'This forgiveness,' says Mr. Yeats, 'was not the forgiveness of the theologian who has received a commandment from afar off, but of the poet and artist, who believes he has been taught, in a mystical vision, "that the imagination is the man himself," and believes he has discovered in the practice of his art that without a perfect sympathy there is no perfect imagination, and therefore no perfect life.' He trusted the passions, because they were alive; and, like Nietzsche, hated asceticism, because

> 'Abstinence sows sand all over
>   The ruddy limbs and flaming hair,
> But desire gratified
>   Plants fruits of life and beauty there.'

'Put off holiness,' he said, 'and put on intellect.' And 'the fool shall not enter into heaven, let him be ever so holy.' Is not this a heaven after the heart of Nietzsche?

Nietzsche is a Spinoza *à rebours*. The essence of the individual, says Spinoza, 'is the effort by which it endeavours to persevere in its own being.' 'Will and understanding are one and the same.' 'By virtue and power I understand the same thing.' 'The effort to understand is the first and sole basis of virtue.' So far it might be Nietzsche who is speaking. Only, in Spinoza, this affirmation of will, persistent egoism, power, hard understanding, leads to a conclusion which is far enough from the conclusion of Neitzsche. 'The absolute virtue of the mind is to understand; its highest virtue, therefore, to understand or know God.' That, to Nietzsche, is one of 'the beautiful words by which the conscience is lulled to sleep.' 'Virtue is power,' Spinoza leads us to think, because it is virtue; 'power is virtue,' affirms Nietzsche, because it is power. And in Spinoza's profound heroism of the mind, really a great humility, 'he who loves God does not desire that God should love him in return,' Nietzsche would find the material for a kind of desperate heroism, made up wholly of pride and defiance.

To Blake, 'God intoxicated' more than Spinoza, 'God only acts and is,' in existing beings and men,' as Spinoza might also have said; to him, as to Spinoza, all moral virtue is identical with understanding, and 'men are admitted into heaven, not because they have curbed and governed their passions, but because they have cultivated their understandings.' Yet to Blake Spinoza's mathematical approach to truth would have been a kind of negation. Even an argument from reason seemed to him atheistical: to one who had truth, as he was assured, within him, reason was only 'the bound or outward circumference of energy,' but 'energy is the only life,' and, as to Nietzsche, is 'eternal delight.'

Yet, to Nietzsche, with his strange, scientific distrust of the imagination, of those who so 'suspiciously' say, 'We see what others do not see,' there comes distrust, hesitation, a kind of despair, precisely at the point where Blake enters into his liberty. 'The habits of our senses,' says Nietzsche, 'have plunged us into the lies and deceptions of feeling.' 'Whoever believes in nature,' says Blake, 'disbelieves in God; for nature is the work of the Devil.' 'These again,' Nietzsche goes on, 'are the foundations of all our judgments and "knowledge," there is no escape whatever, no back-way or by-way into the real world.' But the real world, to Blake, into which he can escape at every moment, is the world of imagination, from which messengers come to him, daily and nightly.

Blake said, 'The tigers of wrath are wiser than the horses of instruction,' and it is partly in what they helped to destroy that Blake and Nietzsche are at one; but destruction, with Blake, was the gesture of a hand which brushes aside needless hindrances, while to Nietzsche it was 'an intellectual thing,' the outer militant part of 'the silent, self-sufficient man in the midst of a general enslavement, who practises self-defence against the outside world, and is constantly living in a state of supreme fortitude.' Blake rejoins Nietzsche as he had rejoined Spinoza, by a different road, having fewer devils to cast out, and no difficulty at all in maintaining his spiritual isolation, his mental liberty, under all circumstances. And to Blake, 'to be 'myself alone, shut up in myself' was to be in no merely individual but in a universal world, that world of imagination whose gates seemed to him to be open to every human being. No less than Nietzsche he says to every man: Be yourself, nothing else matters or exists; but to be myself, to him, was to enter by the imagination into eternity.

The philosophy of Nietzsche was made out of his nerves and was suffering, but to Blake it entered like sunlight into the eyes. Nietzsche's mind is the most sleepless of minds; with him every sensation turns instantly into the stuff of thought; he is terribly alert, the more so because he never stops to systematize; he must be for ever apprehending. He darts out feelers in every direction, relentlessly touching the whole substance of the world. His apprehension is minute rather than broad; he is content to seize one thing at a time, and he is content if each separate thing remains separate; no theory ties together or limits his individual intuitions. What we call his philosophy is really no more than the aggregate of these intuitions coming to us through the medium of a remarkable personality. His personality stands to him in the place of a system. Speaking of Kant and Schopenhauer, he says: 'Their thoughts do not constitute a passionate history of the soul.' His thoughts are the passionate history of his soul. It is for this reason that he is an artist among philosophers rather than a pure philosopher. And remember that he is also not, in the absolute sense, the poet, but the artist. He saw and dreaded the weaknesses of the artist, his side-issues in the pursuit of truth. But in so doing he dreaded one of his own weaknesses.

Blake, on the other hand, receives nothing through his sensations, suffers nothing through his nerves. 'I know of no other Christianity,' he says, 'and of no other Gospel than the liberty both of body and mind to exercise the Divine Arts of Imagination: Imagination, the real and eternal World of which this Vegetable Universe is but a faint shadow, and in which we shall live in our eternal or Imaginative Bodies, when these Vegetable Mortal Bodies are no more.' To Nietzsche the sense of a divine haunting became too heavy a burden for his somewhat inhuman solitude, the solitude of Alpine regions, with their, steadfast glitter, their thin, high, intoxicating air. 'Is this obtrusiveness of heaven,' he cries, 'this inevitable superhuman neighbour, not enough to drive one mad?' But Blake, when he says, 'I am under the direction of messengers from heaven, daily and nightly,' speaks out of natural joy, which is wholly humility, and it is only 'if we fear to do the dictates of our angels, and tremble at the tasks set before us,' it is only then that he dreads, as the one punishment, that 'every one in eternity will leave him.'

II

'There are three powers in man of conversing with Paradise,' said Blake, and he defined them as the three sons of Noah who survived the flood, and who are Poetry, Painting, and Music, Through all three powers, and to the last moments of his life on earth, Blake conversed with Paradise. We are told that he used to sing his own songs to his own music, and that, when he was dying, 'he composed and uttered songs to his Maker,' and 'burst out into singing of the things he saw in heaven.' And with almost the last strength of his hands he had made a sketch of his wife before he 'made the rafters ring,' as a bystander records, with the improvisation of his last breath.

Throughout life his desire had been, as he said, 'to converse with my friends in eternity, see visions, dream dreams, and prophesy and speak parables unobserved.' He says again:

'I rest not from my great task
To open the eternal worlds, to open the immortal eyes
Of Man inwards into the worlds of thought, into eternity,
Ever expanding in the bosom of God, the human imagination.'

And, writing to the uncomprehending Hayley (who had called him 'gentle, visionary Blake'), he says again: 'I am really drunk with intellectual vision whenever I take a pencil or graver into my hand.' To the newspapers of his time, on the one or two occasions when they mentioned his name, he was 'an unfortunate lunatic'; even to Lamb, who looked upon him as 'one of the most extraordinary persons of the age,' he was a man 'flown, whither I know not—to Hades or a madhouse.' To the first editor of his collected poems there seemed to be 'something in his mind not exactly sane'; and the critics of to-day still discuss his sanity as a man and as a poet.

It is true that Blake was abnormal; but what was abnormal in him was his sanity. To one who believed that, 'The ruins of Time build mansions in eternity,' that 'imagination is eternity,' and that 'our deceased friends are more really with us than when they were apparent to our mortal part,' there could be none of that confusion at the edge of mystery which makes a man mad because he is unconscious of the gulf. No one was ever more conscious than Blake was of the limits of that region which we call reality and of that other region which we call imagination.

It pleased him to reject the one and to dwell in the other, and his choice was not the choice of most men, but of some of those who have been the greatest saints and the greatest artists. And, like the most authentic among them, he walked firmly among those realities to which he cared to give no more than a side-glance from time to time; he lived his own life quietly and rationally, doing always exactly what he wanted to do, and with so fine a sense of the subtlety of mere worldly manners, than when, at his one moment of worldly success, in 1793, he refused the post of drawing-master to the royal family, he gave up all his other pupils at the same time, lest the refusal should seem ungracious on the part of one who had been the friend of revolutionaries. He saw visions, but not as the spiritualists and the magicians have seen them. These desire to quicken mortal sight until the soul limits itself again, takes body, and returns to reality; but Blake, the inner mystic, desired only to quicken that imagination which he knew to be more real than the reality of nature. Why should he call up shadows when he could talk in the spirit with spiritual realities? 'Then I asked,' he says in *The Marriage of Heaven and Hell*, 'does a firm persuasion that a thing is so, make it so?' He replied, 'All poets believe that it does.'

In the *Descriptive Catalogue* to his exhibition of pictures in 1809, Blake defines, more precisely than in any other place, what vision was to him. He is speaking of his pictures, but it is a plea for the raising of painting to the same 'sphere of invention and visionary conception' as that which poetry and music inhabit. 'The Prophets,' he says, 'describe what they saw in vision as real and existing men, whom they saw with their imaginative and immortal organs; the Apostles the same; the clearer the organ, the more distinct the object. A spirit and a vision are not, as the modern philosophy supposes, a cloudy vapour, or a nothing. They are organised and minutely articulated beyond all that the mortal and perishing nature can produce. He who does not imagine in stronger and better lineaments and in stronger and better light than his perishing and mortal eye can see, does not imagine at all. The painter of this work asserts that all his imaginations appear to him infinitely more perfect and more minutely organised than anything seen by his mortal eye.' 'Inspiration and vision,' he says in one of the marginal notes to Reynolds's *Discourses*, 'was then, and now is, and I hope will always remain, my element, my eternal dwelling-place.' And 'God forbid,' he says also, 'that Truth should be confined to mathematical demonstration. He who does not know Truth at sight is not worthy of her notice.'

The mind of Blake lay open to eternity as a seed-plot lies open to the sower. In 1802 he writes to Mr. Butts from Felpham: 'I am not ashamed, afraid, or averse to tell you what ought to be told—that I am under the direction of messengers from heaven, daily and nightly.' 'I have written this poem,' he says of the *Jerusalem*, 'from immediate dictation, twelve or sometimes twenty or thirty lines at a time, without premeditation, and even against my will.' 'I may praise it,' he says in another letter, 'since I dare not pretend to be any other than the secretary; the authors are in eternity.' In these words, the most precise claim for direct inspiration which Blake ever made, there is nothing different in kind, only in degree, from what must be felt by every really creative artist and by every profoundly and simply religious person. There can hardly be a poet who is not conscious of how little his own highest powers are under his own control. The creation of beauty is the end of art, but the artist should rarely admit to himself that such is his purpose. A poem is not written by the man who says: I will sit down and write a poem; but rather by the man who, captured by rather than capturing an impulse, hears a tune which he does not recognize, or sees a sight which he does not remember, in some 'close corner of his brain,' and exerts the only energy at his disposal in recording it faithfully, in the medium of his particular art. And so in every creation of beauty, some obscure desire stirred in the soul, not realized by the mind for what it was, and, aiming at most other things in the world than pure beauty, produced it. Now, to the critic this is not more important to remember than it is for him to remember that the result, the end, must be judged, not by the impulse which brought it into being, nor by the purpose which it sought to serve, but by its success or failure in one thing—the creation of beauty. To the artist himself this precise consciousness of what he has done is not always given, any more than a precise consciousness of what he is doing. Only in the greatest do we find vision and the correction of vision equally powerful and equally constant.

To Blake, as to some artists and to most devout people, there was nothing in vision to correct, nothing even to modify. His language in all his letters and in much of his printed work is identical with the language used by the followers of Wesley and

Whitefield at the time in which he was writing. In Wesley's *journal* you will find the same simple and immediate consciousness of the communion of the soul with the world of spiritual reality: not a vague longing, like Shelley's, for a principle of intellectual beauty, nor an unattained desire after holiness, like that of the conventionally religious person, but a literal 'power of conversing with Paradise,' as Blake called it, and as many Methodists would have been equally content to call it. And in Blake, as in those whom the people of that age called 'enthusiasts' (that word of reproach in the eighteenth century and of honour in all other centuries), there was no confusion (except in brains where 'true superstition,' as Blake said, was 'ignorant honesty, and this is beloved of God and man') between the realities of daylight and these other realities from the other side of day. Messrs. Ellis and Yeats quote a mysterious note written in Blake's handwriting, with a reference to Spurzheim, page 154. I find that this means Spurzheim's *Observations on the Deranged Manifestations of the Mind, or Insanity* (1817), and the passage in the text is as follows: 'Religion is another fertile cause of insanity. Mr. Haslam, though he declares it sinful to consider religion as a cause of insanity, adds, however, that he would be ungrateful, did he not avow his obligations to Methodism for its supply of numerous cases. Hence the primitive feelings of religion may be misled and produce insanity; that is what I would contend for, and in that sense religion often leads to insanity.' Blake has written: 'Methodism, etc., p. 154. Cowper came to me and said: "Oh! that I were insane, always. I will never rest. Can not you make me truly insane? I will never rest till I am so. Oh! that in the bosom of God I was hid. You retain health and yet are mad as any of us all—over us all—mad as a refuge from unbelief—from Bacon, Newton, and Locke."' What does this mean but that 'madness,' the madness of belief in spiritual things, must be complete if it is to be effectual, and that, once complete, there is no disturbance of bodily or mental health, as in the doubting and distracted Cowper, who was driven mad, not by the wildness of his belief, but by the hesitations of his doubt?

Attempts have been made to claim Blake for an adept of magic. But whatever cabbalistical terms he may have added to the somewhat composite and fortuitous naming of his mythology ('all but names of persons and places,' he says, 'is invention, both in poetry and painting '), his whole mental attitude was opposed to that of the practisers of magic. We have no record of his ever having evoked a vision, but only of his accepting or enduring visions. Blake was, above all, spontaneous: the practiser of magic is a deliberate craftsman in the art of the soul. I can no more imagine Blake sitting down to juggle with symbols or to gaze into a pool of ink than I can imagine him searching out words that would make the best effects in his lyrics, or fishing for inspiration, pen in hand, in his own ink-pot. A man does not beg at the gate of dreams when he is the master for whose entrance the gate stands open.

Of the definite reality of Blake's visions there can be no question; no question that, as he once wrote, 'nothing can withstand the fury of my course among the stars of God, and in the abysses of the accuser.' But imagination is not one, but manifold; and the metaphor, professing to be no more than metaphor, of the poet, may be vision as essential as the thing actually seen by the visionary. The difference between imagination in Blake and in, say, Shakespeare, is that the one (himself a painter) has a visual imagination and sees an image or metaphor as a literal reality, while the other, seeing it not less vividly but in a more purely mental way, adds a 'like' or an 'as,' and the image or metaphor comes to you with its apology or attenuation, and takes you less by surprise. But to Blake it was the universe that was a metaphor.

CHAPTER I

The origin of the family of William Blake has not yet been found; and I can claim no more for the evidence that I have been able to gather than that it settles us more firmly in our ignorance. But the names of his brothers and sister, their dates and order of birth, and the date of his wife's birth, have never, so far as I know, been correctly given. Even the date of his own birth has been contested by Swinburne 'on good MS. authority,' which we know to be that of Frederick Tatham, who further asserts, wrongly, that James was younger than William, and that John was 'the eldest son.' Gilchrist makes no reference to John, but says, wrongly, that James was 'a year and a half William's senior,' and that William had a sister 'nearly seven years younger than himself; of whom, says Mr. Yeats, 'we hear little, and among that little not even her name.' Most of these problems can be settled by the entries in parish registers, and I have begun with the registers of the church of St. James, Westminster.

I find by these entries that James Blake, the son of James and Catherine Blake, was born July 10, and christened July 15, 1753; John Blake ('son of John and Catherine,' says the register, by what is probably a slip of the pen) was born May 12, and christened June 1, 1755; William Blake was born November 28, and christened December 11, 1757; another John Blake was born March 20, and christened March 30, 1760; Richard Blake was born June 19, and christened July 11, 1762; and Catherine Elizabeth Blake was born January 7, and christened January 28, 1764. Here, where we find the daughter's name and the due order of births, we find one perplexity in the name of Richard, whose date of birth fits the date given by Gilchrist and others to Robert, William's favourite brother, whose name he has engraved on a design of his 'spiritual form' in *Jerusalem*, whom he refers to continually as Robert, and whom J.T. Smith recalls not only as Robert, but as 'Bob, as he was familiarly called.' In the entry of 'John, son of John and Catherine

Blake,' I can easily imagine the clerk repeating by accident the name of the son for the name of the father; and I am inclined to suppose that there was a John who died before the age of five, and that his name was given to the son next born. Precisely the same repetition of name is found in the case of Lamb's two sisters christened Elizabeth, and Shelley's two sisters christened Helen. 'My brother John, the evil one,' would therefore be younger than William; but Tatham, in saying that he was older, may have been misled by there having been two sons christened John.

There are two theories as to the origin of Blake's family; but neither of them has yet been confirmed by the slightest documentary evidence. Both of these theories were put forth in the same year, 1893, one by Mr. Alfred T. Story in his *William Blake*, the other by Messrs. Ellis and Yeats in their *Works of William Blake*. According to Mr. Story, Blake's family was connected with the Somerset family of the Admiral, through a Wiltshire family of Blakes; but for this theory he gives merely the report of 'two ladies, daughters of William John Blake, of Southampton, who claim to be second cousins of William Blake,' and in a private letter he tells me that he has not been able to procure any documentary evidence of the statement. According to Messrs. Ellis and Yeats, Blake's father was Irish, and was originally called O'Neil. His father, John O'Neil, is supposed to have changed his name, on marrying Ellen Blake, from O'Neil to Blake, and James O'Neil, his son by a previous union, to have taken the same name, and to have settled in London, while a younger son, the actual son of Ellen Blake, went to Malaga. This statement rests entirely on the assertion of Dr. Carter Blake, who claimed descent from the latter; and it has never been supported by documentary evidence.

In answer to my inquiry, Mr. Martin J. Blake, the compiler of two volumes of *Blake Family Records* (first series, 1300–1600; second series, 1600–1700), writes: 'Although I have made a special study of the genealogies of the Blakes of Ireland, I have not come across any Ellen Blake who married John O'Neil who afterwards (as is said by Messrs. Ellis and Yeats) adopted the surname of Blake.'

Mr. Sampson points out that Blake's father was certainly a Protestant. He is sometimes described as a Swed-enborgian, always as a Dissenter, and it is curious that about half of the Blakes recorded in the *Dictionary of National Biography* were also conspicuous as Puritans or Dissenters. Mr. Sampson further points out that Blake in one of his poems speaks of himself as 'English

Blake.' It is true that he is contrasting himself with the German Klopstock; yet I scarcely think an Irishman would have used the expression even for contrast. Blake is nowhere referred to as having been in any way Irish, and the only apparent exception to this is one which I am obliged to set up with one hand and knock down with the other. In the index to Crabb Robinson's *Diary* one of the references to Blake shows us Mr. Sheil speaking at the Academical Society while 'Blake, his countryman, kept watching him to keep him in order.' That this does not refer to William Blake I have found by tracking through the unpublished portions of the *Diary* in the original manuscript the numerous references to 'a Mr. Blake' who was accustomed to speak at the meetings of the Academical Society. He is described as 'a Mr. Blake who spoke with good sense on the Irish side, and argued from the Irish History and the circumstances which attended the passing of the bills.' He afterwards speaks 'sharply and coarsely,' and answers Mr. Robinson's hour-long contention that the House of Commons should, or should not, 'possess the power of imprisoning for a breach of privilege,' by 'opposing the facts of Lord Melville's prosecution, the Reversion Bill, etc., etc., and Burke's Reform Bill'; returning, in short, 'my civility by incivility.' This was not the learning, nor were these the manners, of William Blake.

'I would again appeal to the evidence of the parish register. I find Blakes in the parish of St. James, West-minster, from the beginning of the eighteenth century, the first being a William Blake, the son of Richard and Elizabeth, who was born March 19, 1700. Between the years 1750 and 1767 (the time exactly parallel with the births of the family of James and Catherine Blake) I find among the baptisms the names of Frances, Daniel, Reuben, John Cartwright, and William (another William) Blake; and I find among the marriages, between 1728 and 1747, a Robert, a Thomas, a James, and a Richard Blake. The wife of James, who was married on April 15, 1738, is called Elizabeth, a name which we have already found as the name of a Mrs. Blake, and which we find again as the second name of Catherine Elizabeth Blake (the sister of William Blake), who was born in 1764. I find two Williams, two Richards, and a John among the early entries, at the beginning of the eighteenth century. It is impossible to say positively that any of these families, not less than nine in number, all bearing the name of Blake, all living in the same parish, within a space of less than forty years, were related to one another; but it is easier to suppose so than to suppose that one only out of the number, and one which had assumed the name, should have found itself accidentally in the midst of all the others to which the name may be supposed to have more definitely belonged.

All that we know with certainty of James Blake, the father, is that he was a hosier ('of respectable trade and easy habits,' says Tatham; 'of fifty years' standing,' says Cunningham, at the time of his death), that he was a Dissenter (a Swedenborgian, or inclined to Swedenborgianism), and that he died in 1784 and was buried on July 4 in Bunhill Fields. The burial register says: 'July 4, 1784. Mr. James Blake from Soho Square in a grave, 13/6.' Of his wife Catherine all that we know is that she died in 1792, and was also buried in Bunhill Fields. The register says: 'Sept. 9, 1792. Catherine Blake; age 70; brought from St. James, Westminster. Grave 9 feet; E. & W. 16; N. & S. 42–43. 19/–.' Tatham says that 'even when a child, his mother beat him for running and saying that he saw the prophet Ezekiel under a tree in the fields.' At eight or ten he comes home from Peckham Rye saying that he has seen a tree filled with angels; and his father is going to beat him for telling a lie; but his mother intercedes. It was the father, Tatham says, who, noticing to what great anger he was moved by a blow, decided not to send him to school.

The eldest son, James, Tatham tells us, 'having a saving, somniferous mind, lived a yard and a half life, and pestered his brother with timid sentences of bread and cheese advice.' On his father's death in 1784 he carried on the business, and it was at his house that Blake held his one exhibition of pictures in 1809. 'These paintings filled several rooms of an ordinary dwelling-house,' says Crabb Robinson in his *Reminiscences*; and, telling how he had bought four copies of the catalogue, 'giving 10/–, I bargained that I should be at liberty to go again.' 'Free!, as long as you live!' said the brother, astonished at such a liberality, which he had never experienced before nor I dare say did afterwards. Crabb Robinson had at first written 'as long as you like,' and this he altered into 'as long as you live,' as if fancying, so long afterwards as 1852, that he remembered the exact word; but in the entry in the *Diary*, in 1810, we read 'Oh! as often as you please!' so that we may doubt whether the 'honest, unpretending shopkeeper,' who was looked upon by his neighbours, we are told, as 'a bit mad,' because he would talk 'Swedenborg,' can be credited with all the enthusiasm of the later and more familiar reading. James and William no longer spoke to one another when, after retiring from business, James came to live in Cirencester Street, near Linnell. Tatham tells us that 'he got together a little annuity, upon which he supported his only sister, and vegetating to a moderate age, died about three years before his brother William.'

Of John we know only that he was something of a scapegrace and the favourite son of his parents. He was apprenticed, at some cost, to a candle-maker, but ran away, and, after some help from William, enlisted in the army, lived wildly, and died young. Robert, the favourite of William, also died young, at the age of twenty-five. He lived with William and Catherine from 1784 to the time of his death in 1787, at 27 Broad Street, helping in the print-shop of 'Parker & Blake,' and learning from his brother to draw and engrave. One of his original sketches, a stiff drawing of long, rigid, bearded figures staring in terror, quite in his brother's manner, is in the Print Room of the British Museum. A story is told of him by Gilchrist which gives us the whole man, indeed the whole household, in brief. There had been a dispute between him and Mrs. Blake. Blake suddenly interposed, and said to his wife: 'Kneel down and beg Robert's pardon directly, or you will never see my face again.' She knelt down (thinking it, as she said afterwards, 'very hard,' for she felt herself to be in the right) and said: 'Robert, I beg your pardon; I am in the wrong.' 'Young woman, you lie,' said Robert, 'I am in the wrong.'

Early in 1787 Robert fell ill, and during the last fortnight William nursed him without taking rest by day or night, until, at the moment of death, he saw his brother's soul rise through the ceiling 'clapping its hands for joy'; whereupon he went to bed and slept for three days and nights. Robert was buried in Bunhill Fields on February 11. The register says: 'Feb. 11, 1787. Mr. Robert Blake from Golden Square in a grave, 13/6.' But his spiritual presence was never to leave the mind of William Blake, who in 1800 we find writing to Hayley: 'Thirteen years ago I lost a brother, and with his spirit I converse daily and hourly in the spirit, and see him in remembrance, in the regions of my imagination. I hear his advice, and even now write from his dictate.' It was Robert whom he saw in a dream, not long after his death, telling him the method by which he was to engrave his poems and designs. The spiritual forms of William and of Robert, in almost exact parallel, are engraved on separate pages of the Prophetic Book of *Milton*.

Of the sister, Catherine Elizabeth, we know only that she lived with Blake and his wife at Felpham. He refers to her in several letters, and in the poem sent to Butts on October 2, 1800, he speaks of her as 'my sister and friend.' In another poem, sent to Butts in a letter dated November 22, 1802, but written, he explains, 'above a twelvemonth ago, while walking from Felpham to Lavant to meet my sister,' he asks strangely:

> 'Must my wife live in my sister's bane,
> Or my sister survive on my Love's pain?'

but from the context it is not clear whether this is meant literally or figuratively. When Tatham was writing his life of Blake, apparently in the year 1831, he refers to 'Miss Catherine' as still living, 'having survived nearly all her relations.' Mrs. Gilchrist, in a letter written to Mr. W.M. Rossetti in 1862, reports a rumour, for which she gives no evidence, that 'she and Mrs. Blake got on very ill together, and latterly never met at all,' and that she died in extreme penury.

CHAPTER II

Of the childhood and youth of Blake we know little beyond what Malkin and Smith have to tell us. From the age of ten to the age of fourteen he studied at Pars' drawing-school in the Strand, buying for himself prints after Raphael, Dürer, and Michelangelo at tne sale-rooms; at fourteen he was apprenticed to Basire, the engraver, who lived at 31 Great Queen Street, and in his shop Blake once saw Goldsmith. 'His love for art increasing,' says Tatham, 'and the time of life having arrived when it was deemed necessary to place him under some tutor, a painter of eminence was proposed, and necessary applications were made; but from the huge premium required, he requested, with his characteristic generosity, that his father would not on any account spend so much money on him, as he thought it would be an injustice to his brothers and sisters. He therefore himself proposed engraving as being less expensive, and sufficiently eligible for his future avocations. Of Basire, therefore, for a premium of fifty guineas, he learnt the art of engraving.' We are told that he was apprenticed, at his own request, to Basire rather than to the more famous Ryland, the engraver to the king, because, on being taken by his father to Ryland's studio, he said: 'I do not like the man's face: it looks as if he will live to be hanged.' Twelve years later Ryland was hanged for forgery.

Blake was with Basire for seven years, and for the last five years much of his time was spent in making drawings of Gothic monuments, chiefly in Westminster Abbey, until he came, says Malkin, to be 'himself almost a Gothic monument.' Tatham tells us that the reason of his being 'sent out drawing,' as he fortunately was, instead of being kept at engraving, was 'for the circumstance of his having frequent quarrels with his fellow-apprentices concerning matters of intellectual argument.'

It was in the Abbey that he had a vision of Christ and the Apostles, and in the Abbey, too, that he flung an intrusive

Westminster schoolboy from the scaffolding, 'in the impetuosity of his anger, worn out with interruption,' says Tatham, and then laid a complaint before the Dean which has caused, to this day, the exclusion of Westminster schoolboys from the precincts.

It was at this time that Blake must have written the larger part of the poems contained in the *Poetical Sketches*, printed (we cannot say published) in 1783, for in the 'Advertisement' at the beginning of the book we are told that the 'following Sketches were the production of untutored youth, commenced in his twelfth, and occasionally resumed by the author till his twentieth, year,' that is to say, between the years 1768 and 1777. The earliest were written while Goldsmith and Gray were still living, the latest (if we may believe these dates) after Chatterton's death, but before his poems had been published. Ossian had appeared in 1760, Percy's *Reliques* in 1765. The *Reliques* probably had their influence on Blake, Ossian certainly, an influence which returns much later, curiously mingled with the influence of Milton, in the form taken by the Prophetic Books. It has been suggested that some of Blake's mystical names, and his 'fiend in a cloud,' came from Ossian; and Ossian is very evident in the metrical prose of such pieces as 'Samson,' and even in some of the imagery ('Their helmed youth and aged warriors in dust together lie, and Desolation spreads his wings over the land of Palestine'). But the influence of Chatterton seems not less evident, an influence which could hardly have found its way to Blake before the year 1777. In the fifth chapter of the fantastic *Island in the Moon* (probably written about 1784) there is a long discussion on Chatterton, while in the seventh chapter he is again discussed in company with Homer, Shakespeare, and Milton. As late as 1826 Blake wrote on the margin of Wordsworth's preface to the *Lyrical Ballads*: 'I believe both Macpherson and Chatterton that what they say is ancient is so,' and on another page, 'I own myself an admirer of Ossian equally with any poet whatever, of Rowley and Chatterton also.' Whether it be influence or affinity, it is hard to say, but if the 'Mad Song' of Blake has the hint of any predecessor in our literature, it is to be found in the abrupt energy and stormy masculine splendour of the High Priest's song in '*Aella*,' 'Ye who hie yn mokie ayre'; and if, between the time of the Elizabethans and the time of 'My silks and fine array' there had been any other song of similar technique and similar imaginative temper, it was certainly the Minstrel's song in '*Aella*,' 'O! synge untoe mie roundelaie.'

Of the direct and very evident influence of the Elizabethans we are told by Malkin, with his quaint preciseness: 'Shakespeare's *Venus and Adonis, Tarquin and Lucrece,* and his *Sonnets* ... poems, now little read, were favourite studies of Mr. Blake's early days. So were Jonson's *Underwoods* and his *Miscellanies.*' 'My silks and fine array' goes past Jonson, and reaches Fletcher, if not Shakespeare himself. And the blank verse of 'King Edward the Third' goes straight to Shakespeare for its cadence, and for something of its manner of speech. And there is other blank verse which, among much not even metrically correct, anticipates something of the richness of Keats.

Some rags of his time did indeed cling about him, but only by the edges; there is even a reflected ghost of the pseudo-Gothic of Walpole in 'Fair Elenor,' who comes straight from the *Castle of Otranto,* as 'Gwin, King of Norway,' takes after the Scandinavian fashion of the day, and may have been inspired by *The Fatal Sisters* or *The Triumphs of Owen* of Gray. 'Blindman's Buff,' too, is a piece of eighteenth-century burlesque realism. But it is in the ode 'To the Muses' that Blake for once accepts, and in so doing clarifies, the smooth convention of eighteenth-century classicism, and, as he reproaches it in its own speech, illuminates it suddenly with the light it had rejected:

> 'How have you left the ancient love
> That bards of old enjoyed in you!
> The languid strings do scarcely move,
> The sound is forced, the notes are few!'

In those lines the eighteenth century dies to music, and from this time forward we find in the rest of Blake's work only a proof of his own assertion, that 'the ages are all equal; but genius is above the age.'

In 1778 Blake's apprenticeship to Basire came to an end, and for a short time he studied in the Antique School at the newly founded Royal Academy under Moser, the first keeper. In the Life of Reynolds which prefaces the 1798 edition of the *Discourses,* Moser is spoken of as one who 'might in every sense be called the Father of the present race of Artists.' Blake has written against this in his copy: 'I was once looking over the prints from Raphael and Michael Angelo in the Library of the Royal Academy. Moser came to me and said, "You should not study these old hard, stiff, and

Dry Unfinished Works of Art. Stay a little, and I will show you what you should study." He then went and took down Le Brun's and Rubens' Galleries. How did I secretly rage. I also spoke my mind. I said to Moser, "These things that you call Finished are not even Begun: how can they then be Finished? The man who does not know the Beginning never can know the end of Art."' Malkin tells us that Blake 'professed drawing from life always to have been hateful to him; and speaks of it as looking more like death, or smelling of mortality. Yet still he drew a good deal from life, both at the Academy and at home.' A water-colour drawing dating from this time, 'The Penance of Jane Shore,' was included by Blake in his exhibition of 1809. It is the last number in the catalogue, and has the note: 'This Drawing was done above Thirty Years ago, and proves to the Author, and he thinks will prove to any discerning eye, that the productions of our youth and of our maturer age are equal in all essential respects.' He also did engravings, during several years, for the booksellers, Harrison, Johnson, and others, some of them after Stothard, who was then working for the *Novelist's Magazine*. Blake met Stothard in 1780, and Stothard introduced him to Flaxman, with whom he had himself just become acquainted. In the same year Blake met Fuseli, who settled near him in Broad Street, while Flaxman, on his marriage in 1781, came to live near by, at 27 Wardour Street. Bartolozzi and John Varley were both, then or later, living in Broad Street, Angelica Kauffmann in Golden Square. In 1780 (the year of the Gordon Riots, when Blake, carried along by the crowd, saw the burning of Newgate) he had for the first time a picture in the Royal Academy, the water-colour of 'The Death of Earl Godwin.'

It was at this time, in his twenty-fourth year, that he fell in love with 'a lively little girl' called Polly Wood. Tatham calls her 'a young woman, who by his own account, and according to his own knowledge, was no trifler. He wanted to marry her, but she refused, and was as obstinate as she was unkind.' Gilchrist says that on his complaining to her that she had 'kept company' with others besides himself, she asked him if he was a fool. 'That cured me of jealousy,' he said afterwards, but the cure, according to Tatham, made him so ill that he was sent for change of air to 'Kew, near Richmond' (really to Battersea), to the house of 'a market-gardener whose name was Boutcher.' While there, says Tatham, 'he was relating to the daughter, a girl named Catherine, the lamentable story of Polly Wood, his implacable lass, upon which Catherine expressed her deep sympathy, it is supposed, in such a tender and affectionate manner, that it quite won him. He immediately said, with the suddenness peculiar to him, "Do you pity me?" "Yes, indeed I do," answered she. "Then I love you," said he again. Such was their courtship. He was impressed by her tenderness of mind, and her answer indicated her previous feeling for him: for she has often said that upon her mother's asking her who among her acquaintances she could fancy for a husband, she replied that she had not yet seen the man, and she has further been heard to say that when she first came into the room in which Blake sat, she instantly recognized (like Britomart in Merlin's wondrous glass) her future partner, and was so near fainting that she left his presence until she recovered.' Tatham tells us that Blake 'returned to his lodgings and worked incessantly' for a whole year, 'resolving that he would not see her until he had succeeded' in making enough money to be able to marry her. The marriage took place at Battersea in August, 1782.

Gilchrist says that he has traced relatives of Blake to have been living at Battersea at the time of his marriage. Of this he gives no evidence; but I think I have found traces, in Blake's own parish, of relatives of the Catherine Boucher whom he married at Battersea. Tatham, as we have seen, says that she was the daughter of a market-gardener at 'Kew, near Richmond,' called Boutcher, to whose house Blake was sent for a change of air. Allan Cunningham says that 'she lived near his father's house.' I think I have found the reason for Cunningham's mistake, and the probable occasion of Blake's visit to the Bouchers at Battersea. I find by the birth register in St. Mary's, Battersea, that Catherine Sophia, daughter of William and Ann Boucher, was born April 25, and christened May 16, 1762. Four years after this, another Catherine Boucher, daughter of Samuel and Betty, born March 28, 1766, was christened March 31, 1766, in the parish church of St. James, Westminster; and in the same register I find the birth of Gabriel, son of the same parents, born September 1, and christened September 20, 1767; and of Ann, daughter of Thomas and Ann Boucher, born June 12, and christened June 29, 1761. Is it not, therefore, probable that there were Bouchers, related to one another, living in both parishes, and that Blake's acquaintance with the family living near him led to his going to stay with the family living at Battersea?

The entry of Blake's marriage, in the register of St. Mary's, Battersea, gives the name as Butcher, and also describes Blake as 'of the parish of Battersea,' by a common enough error. It is as follows:—

'1782.

'Banns of Marriage.

'No. 281 William Blake of the Parish of Battersea Batchelor and Catherine Butcher of the same Parish Spinster were Married in this Church by License this Eighteenth Day of August in the Year One Thousand Seven Hundred and Eighty Two by me J. Gardnor Vicar. This Marriage was solemnized between Us

William Blake
The mark of X Catherine Butcher

'In the presence of Thomas Monger Butcher

Jas. Blake
Robt. Munday Parish Clerk.'

I imagine that Thomas Monger Butcher was probably Catherine's brother; there are other Mongers not far off in the register, as if the name were a family name. His handwriting is mean and untidy, James Blake's vague but fluent; Catherine makes her mark somewhat faintly. As the register lies open there are entries of seven marriages; out of these, no fewer than three of the brides have signed by making their mark. The name William Blake stands out from these 'blotted and blurred' signatures; the ink is very black, as if he had pressed hard on the pen; and the name has a firm and determinate outline.'

Gilchrist describes Catherine Boucher as 'a bright-eyed, dark-haired brunette, with expressive features and a slim, graceful form.' This seems to be merely a re-writing of Allan Cunningham's vague statement that she 'was noticed by Blake for the whiteness of her hand, the brightness of her eyes, and a slim and handsome shape, corresponding with his own notions of sylphs and naiads.' But if a quaint and lovely pencil sketch in the Rossetti MS., representing a man in bed and a woman sitting on the side of the bed, beginning to dress, is really, as it probably is, done from life, and meant for Mrs. Blake, we see at once the model for his invariable type of woman, tall, slender, and with unusually long legs. There is a drawing of her head by Blake in the Rossetti MS. which, though apparently somewhat conventionalized, shows a clear aquiline profile and very large eyes; still to he divined in the rather painful head drawn by Tatham when she was an old woman, a head in which there is still power and fixity. Crabb Robinson, who met her in 1825, says that she had 'a good expression in her countenance, and, with a dark eye, remains of beauty in her youth.'

No man of genius ever had a better wife. To the last she called him 'Mr. Blake,' while he, we are told, most frequently spoke of her as 'his beloved.' The most beautiful reference to her which I find in his letters is one in a letter of September 16, 1800, to Hayley, where he calls her 'my dear and too careful and over-joyous woman,' and says 'Eartham will be my first temple and altar; my wife is like a flame of many colours of precious jewels whenever she hears it named.' He taught her to write, and her writing, says Gilchrist, is scarcely to be distinguished from his; to draw, so that after his death she finished some of his designs; and to help him in the printing and colouring of his engravings. A story is told, on the authority of Samuel Palmer, that they would both look into the flames of burning coals, and draw grotesque figures which they saw there, hers quite unlike his. 'It is quite certain,' says Crabb Robinson, 'that she believed in all his visions'; and he shows her to us reminding her husband, 'You know, dear, the first time you saw God was when you were four years old, and he put his head to the window, and set you a-screaming.' She would walk with him into the country, whole summer days, says Tatham, and far into the night. And when he rose in the night, to write down what was 'dictated' to him, she would rise and sit by him, and hold his hand. 'She would get up in the night,' says the unnamed friend quoted by Gilchrist, 'when he was under his very fierce inspirations, which were as if they would tear him asunder, while he was yielding himself to the Muse, or whatever else it could be called, sketching and writing. And so terrible a task did this seem to be, that she had to sit motionless and silent; only to stay him mentally, without moving hand or foot; this for hours, and night after night.' 'His wife being to him a very patient woman,' says Tatham, who speaks of Mrs. Blake as 'an irradiated saint,' 'he fancied that while she looked on him as he worked, her sitting quite still by his side, doing nothing, soothed his impetuous mind; and he has many a time, when a strong desire presented itself to overcome any difficulty in his plates or drawings, in the middle of the night, risen, and requested her to get up with him, and sit by his side, in which she as cheerfully acquiesced.' 'Rigid, punctual, firm, precise,' she has been described; a good housewife and a good cook; refusing to have a servant not, only because of the cost, but because no servant could be scrupulous enough to satisfy her. 'Finding,' says Tatham '(as Mrs. Blake declared, and as every one else knows), 'the more service the more inconvenience, she... did all the work herself, kept the house clean and herself tidy, besides printing all Blake's numerous engravings, which was a task sufficient for any industrious woman.' He tells us in another place: 'it is a fact known to the writer, that Mrs. Blake's frugality always kept a guinea or sovereign for any emergency, of which Blake never knew, even to the day of his death.'

Tatham says of Blake at the time of his marriage: 'Although not handsome, he must have had a most noble countenance, full of expression and animation; his hair was of a yellow brown, and curled with the utmost crispness and luxuriance; his locks, instead of falling down, stood up like a curling flame, and looked at a distance like radiations, which with his fiery eye and expressive forehead, his dignified and cheerful physiognomy, must have made his appearance truly prepossessing.' In another place he says: 'William Blake in stature was short [he was not quite five and a half feet in height], but well made, and very well proportioned; so much so that West, the great history painter, admired much the form of his limbs; he had a large head and wide shoulders. Elasticity and promptitude of action were the characteristics of his contour. His motions were rapid and energetic, betokening a mind filled with elevated enthusiasm; his forehead was very high and prominent over the frontals; his eye most unusually large and glassy, with which he appeared to look into some other world.' His eyes were prominent, 'large, dark, and expressive,' says Allan Cunningham; the flashing of his eyes remained in the memory of an old man who had seen him in court at Chichester in 1804. His nose, though 'snubby,' as he himself describes it, had 'a little clenched nostril, a nostril that opened as far as it could, but was tied down at the end.' The mouth was large and sensitive; the forehead, larger below than above, as he himself noted, was broad and high; and the whole face, as one sees it in what is probably the best likeness we have, Linnell's miniature of 1827, was full of irregular splendour, eager, eloquent, ecstatic; eyes and mouth and nostrils all as if tense with a continual suction, drinking up 'large draughts of intellectual day' with impatient haste. 'Infinite impatience,' says Swinburne, as of a great preacher or apostle—intense tremulous vitality, as of a great orator seem to me to give his face the look of one who can do all things but hesitate.'

After his marriage in August, 1782 (which has been said to have displeased his father, though Tatham says it was 'with the approbation and consent of his parents'), Blake took lodgings at 23 Green Street, Leicester Fields (now pulled down), which was only the square's length away from Sir Joshua Reynolds. Flaxman had married in 1781, and had taken a house at 27 Wardour Street; and it was probably he who, about this time, introduced Blake to 'the accomplished Mrs. Matthew,' whose drawing-room in Rathbone Place was frequented by literary and artistic people. Mr. Matthew, a clergyman of taste, who is said to have 'read the church service more beautifully than any other clergyman in London,' had discovered Flaxman, when a little boy, learning Latin behind the counter in his father's shop. 'From this incident,' says J. T. Smith in his notice of Flaxman, 'Mr. Matthew continued to notice him, and, as he grew up, became his first and best friend. Later on, he was introduced to Mrs. Matthew, who was so kind as to read Homer to him, whilst he made designs on the same table with her at the time she was reading. 'It was apparently at the Matthews' house that Smith heard Blake sing his own songs to his own music, and it was through Mrs. Matthew's good opinion of these songs that she 'requested the Rev. Henry Matthew, her husband, to join Mr. Flaxman in his truly kind offer of defraying the expense of printing them': to which we owe the '*Poetical Sketches*, by W. B.'—printed in 1783, and given to Blake to dispose of as he thought fit. There is no publisher's name on the book, and there is no reason to suppose that it was ever offered for sale.

'With his usual urbanity,' Mr. Matthew had written a foolish 'Advertisement' to the book, saying that the author had 'been deprived of the leisure requisite to such a revisal of these sheets, as might have rendered them less unfit to meet the public eye,' 'his talents having been wholly directed to the attainment of excellence in his profession.' The book is by no means incorrectly printed, and it is not probable that Blake would under any circumstances have given his poems more 'revisal' than he did. He did at this time a good deal of engraving, often after the designs of Stothard, whom he was afterwards to accuse of stealing his ideas; and in 1784 he had two, and in 1785 four, water—colour drawings at the Royal Academy. Fuseli, Stothard, and Flaxman[1] seem to have been his chief friends, and it is probable that he also knew Cosway, who practised magic, and Cosway may have told him about Paracelsus, or lent him Law's translation of Boheme, while Flaxman, who was a Swedenborgian, may have brought him still more closely under the influence of Swedenborg.

In any case, he soon tired of the coterie of the Matthews, and we are told that it soon ceased to relish his 'manly firmness of opinion.' What he really thought of it we may know with some certainty from the extravaganza, *An Island in the Moon*, which seems to belong to 1784, and which is a light-hearted and incoherent satire, derived, no doubt, from Sterne, and pointing, as Mr. Sampson justly says, to Peacock. It is unfinished, and was not worth finishing, but it contains the first version of several of the *Songs of Innocence*, as well as the lovely song of Phœbe and Jellicoe. It has the further interest of showing us Blake's first, wholly irresponsible attempt to create imaginary worlds, and to invent grotesque and impossible names. It shows us the first explosions of that inflammable part of his nature, which was to burst through the quiet surface of his life at many intervals, in righteous angers and irrational suspicions. It betrays his deeply rooted dislike of science, and, here and there, a literary preference, for Ossian or for Chatterton. The original MS. is in the Fitzwilliam Museum, Cambridge, and in this year, 1907, Mr. Edwin J. Ellis has done Blake the unkindness of printing it for the first time in full, in the pages of his *Real Blake*. Blake's satire is only occasionally good, though occasionally it is supremely good; his burlesque is almost always bad; and there is little probability that he ever intended to publish any part of the prose and verse which he threw off for the relief of personal irritations and spiritual indignations.

---

1. Compare the lines written in 1800:

'I bless thee, O Father of Heaven and Earth, that ever I saw Flaxman's face.
Angles stand round my spirit in Heaven, the blessed of Heaven are my friends upon Earth.
When Flaxman was taken to Italy, Fuseli was given to me for a season...
And my Angels have told me that seeing such visions, I could not subsist on the Earth,
But my conjunction with Flaxman, who knows to forgive nervous fear.'

In *An Island in the Moon* we see Blake casting off the dust of the drawing-rooms, finally, so far as any mental obstruction was concerned; but he does not seem to have broken wholly with the Matthews, who, no doubt, were people of genuinely good intentions; and it is through their help that we find him, in 1784, on the death of his father, setting up as a print-seller, with his former fellow-apprentice, James Parker, at No. 27 Broad Street, next door to the house and shop which had been his father's, and which were now taken on by his brother James. Smith says that he took a shop and a first-floor; and here his brother Robert came to live with him as his pupil, and remained with him till his death in February, 1787.

CHAPTER III

After Robert's death Blake gave up the print-shop and moved out of Broad Street to Poland Street, a street running between it and Oxford Street. He took No. 28, a house only a few doors down from Oxford Street, and lived there for five years. Here, in 1789, he issued the *Songs of Innocence*, the first of his books to be produced by the method of his invention, which he described as 'illuminated printing.' According to Smith, it was Robert who 'stood before him in one of his visionary imaginations, and directed him in the way in which he ought to proceed.' The process is thus described by Mr. Sampson: 'The text and surrounding design were written in reverse, in a medium impervious to acid, upon small copper-plates, which were then etched in a bath of aqua-fortis until the work stood in relief as in a stereotype. From these plates, which to economize copper were in many cases engraved upon both sides, impressions were printed, in the ordinary manner, in tints made to harmonize with the colour scheme afterwards applied in water-colours by the artist.' Gilchrist tells an improbable story about Mrs. Blake going out with the last half-crown in the house, and spending 1*s*. 10*d*. of it in the purchase of 'the simple materials necessary.' But we know from a MS. note of John Linnell, referring to a somewhat later date: 'The copperplates which Blake engraved to illustrate Hayley's life of Cowper were, as he told me, printed entirely by himself and his wife in his own press—a very good one which cost him forty pounds.' These plates were engraved in 1803, but it is not likely that Blake was ever able to buy more than one press.

The problem of 'illuminated printing,' however definitely it may have been solved by the dream in which Robert 'stood before him and directed him,' was one which had certainly occupied the mind of Blake for some years. A passage, unfortunately incomplete, in *An Island in the Moon*, reads as follows: '..."Illuminating the Manuscript" — "Ay, "said she, "that would be excellent." "Then," said he, "I would have all the writing engraved instead of printed, and at every other leaf a high finished print, all in three volumes folio, and sell them a hundred pounds a piece. They would print off two thousand." "Then," said she, "whoever will not have them, will be ignorant fools and will not deserve to live." This is evidently a foreshadowing of the process which is described and defended, with not less confident enthusiasm, in an engraved prospectus issued from Lambeth in 1793. I give it in full:

'*October* 10, 1793.

'TO THE PUBLIC.

'The Labours of the Artist, the Poet, the Musician, have been proverbially attended by poverty and obscurity; this was never the fault of the Public, but was owing to a neglect of means to propagate such works as have wholly absorbed the Man of Genius. Even Milton and Shakespeare could not publish their own works.

'This difficulty has been obviated by the Author of the following productions now presented to the Public; who has invented a method of Printing both Letter-press and Engraving in a style more ornamental, uniform, and grand, than any before discovered, while it produces works at less than one-fourth of the expense.

'If a method of Printing which combines the Painter and the Poet is a phenomenon worthy of public attention, provided that it exceeds in elegance all former methods, the Author is sure of his reward.

'Mr. Blake's powers of invention very early engaged the attention of many persons of eminence and fortune; by whose means he has been regularly enabled to bring before the public works (he is not afraid to say) of equal magnitude and consequence with the productions of any age or country: among which are two large highly finished engravings (and two more are nearly ready) which will commence a Series of subjects from the Bible, and another from the *History of England*.

'The following are the Subjects of the several Works now published and on Sale at Mr. Blake's, No. 13 Hercules Buildings, Lambeth:—

'1. "Job", a Historical Engraving. Size 1 ft. 7½ in. by 1 ft. 2 in. Price 12s.

'2. "Edward and Elinor", a Historical Engraving. Size 1 ft. 6½ in. by 1 ft. Price 10s. 6d.

'3. *America, a Prophecy*, in Illuminated Printing. Folio, with 18 designs. Price 10s. 6d.

'4. *Visions of the Daughters of Albion*, in Illuminated Printing. Folio, with 8 designs. Price 7s. 6d.

'5. *The Book of Thel*, a Poem in Illuminated Printing. Quarto, with 6 designs. Price 3s.

'6. *The Marriage of Heaven and Hell*, in Illuminated Printing. Quarto, with 14 designs. Price 7s. 6d.

'7. *Songs of Innocence*, in Illuminated Printing. Octavo, with 25 designs. Price 5s.

'8. *Songs of Experience*, in Illuminated Printing. Octavo, with 25 designs. Price 5s.

'9. *The History of England*, a small book of Engravings. Price 3s.

'10. *The Gates of Paradise*, a small book of Engravings. Price 3s.

'The Illuminated Books are Printed in Colours, and on the most beautiful wove paper that could be procured.

'No Subscriptions for the numerous great works now in hand are asked, for none are wanted; but the Author will produce his works, and offer them to sale at a fair price.

By this invention (which it is absurd to consider, as some have considered it, a mere makeshift, to which he had been driven by the refusal of publishers to issue his poems and engravings according to the ordinary trade methods) Blake was the first, and remains the only, poet who has in the complete sense made his own books with his own hands: the words, the illustrations, the engraving, the printing, the colouring, the very inks and colours, and the stitching of the sheets into boards. With Blake, who was equally a poet and an artist, words and designs came together and were inseparable; and to the power of inventing words and designs was added the skill of engraving, and thus of interpreting them, without any mechanical interference from the outside. To do this must have been, at some time or another, the ideal of every poet who is a true artist, and who has a sense of the equal importance of every form of art, and of every detail in every form. Only Blake has produced a book of poems vital alike in inner and outer form, and, had it not been for his lack of a technical knowledge of music, had he but been able to write down his inventions in that art also, he would have left us the creation of something like an universal art. That universal art he did, during his own lifetime, create; for he sang his songs to his own music; and thus, while he lived, he was the complete realization of the poet in all his faculties, and the only complete realization that has ever been known.

To define the poetry of Blake one must find new definitions for poetry; but, these definitions once found, he will seem to be the only poet who is a poet in essence; the only poet who could, in his own words, 'enter into Noah's rainbow, and make a friend and companion of one of these images of wonder, which always entreat him to leave mortal things.' In this verse there is, if it is to be found in any verse, the 'lyrical cry'; and yet, what voice is it that cries in this disembodied ecstasy? The voice of desire is not in it, nor the voice of passion, nor the cry of the heart, nor the cry of the sinner to God, nor of the lover of nature to nature. It neither seeks nor aspires nor laments nor questions. It is like the voice of wisdom in a child, who has not yet forgotten the world out of which the soul came. It is as spontaneous as the note of a bird, it is an affirmation of life; in its song, which seems mere music, it is the mind which sings; it is lyric thought. What is it that transfixes one in any couplet such as this:

> 'If the sun and moon should doubt
> They'd immediately go out'?

It is no more than a nursery statement, there is not even an image in it, and yet it sings to the brain, it cuts into the very flesh of the mind, as if there were a great weight behind it. Is it that it is an arrow, and that it comes from so far, and with an impetus gathered from its speed out of the sky?

The lyric poet, every lyric poet but Blake, sings of love; but Blake sings of forgiveness:

> 'Mutual forgiveness of each vice,
> Such are the gates of Paradise.'

Poets sing of beauty, but Blake says:

> 'Soft deceit and idleness,
> These are Beauty's sweetest dress.'

They sing of the brotherhood of men, but Blake points to the 'divine image':

> 'Cruelty has a human heart,
> And Jealousy a human face;

Terror the human form divine,
And Secrecy the human dress.'

Their minds are touched by the sense of tears in human things, but to Blake 'a tear is an intellectual thing.' They sing of 'a woman like a dewdrop,' but Blake of 'the lineaments of gratified desire.' They shout hymns to God over a field of battle or in the arrogance of material empire; but Blake addresses the epilogue of his *Gates of Paradise* 'to the Accuser who is the God of this world':

'Truly, my Satan, thou art but a dunce,
And dost not know the garment from the man;
Every harlot was a virgin once,
Nor canst thou ever change Kate into Nan.
Though thou art worshipped by the names divine
Of Jesus and Jehovah, thou art still
The son of morn in weary night's decline,
The lost traveller's dream under the hill.'

Other poets find ecstasy in nature, but Blake only in imagination. He addresses the Prophetic Book of *The Ghost of Abel* 'to Lord Byron in the wilderness,' and asks: 'What doest thou here, Elijah? Can a poet doubt of the visions of Jehovah? Nature has no outline, but Imagination has. Nature has no time, but Imagination has. Nature has no supernatural, and dissolves. Imagination is eternity.' The poetry of Blake is a poetry of the mind, abstract in substance, concrete in form; its passion is the passion of the imagination, its emotion is the emotion of thought, its beauty is the beauty of idea. When it is simplest, its simplicity is that of some 'infant joy' too young to have a name, or of some 'infant sorrow' brought aged out of eternity into the 'dangerous world,' and there,

'Helpless, naked, piping loud,
Like a fiend hid in a cloud.'

There are no men and women in the world of Blake's poetry, only primal instincts and the energies of the imagination.

His work begins in the Garden of Eden, or of the childhood of the world, and there is something in it of the naïveté of beasts: the lines gambol awkwardly, like young lambs. His utterance of the state of innocence has in it something of the grotesqueness of babies, and enchants the grown man, as they do. Humour exists unconscious of itself, in a kind of awed and open-eyed solemnity. He stammers into a speech of angels, as if just awakening out of Paradise. It is the primal instincts that speak first, before riper years have added wisdom to intuition. It is the supreme quality of this wisdom that it has never let go of intuition. It is as if intuition itself ripened. And so Blake goes through life with perfect mastery of the terms of existence, as they present themselves to him: 'perfectly happy, wanting nothing,' as he said, when he was old and poor; and able in each stage of life to express in art the corresponding stage of his own development. He is the only poet who has written the songs of childhood, of youth, of mature years, and of old age; and he died singing.

CHAPTER IV

Blake lived in Poland Street for five years, and issued from it the *Songs of Innocence* (1789), and, in the same year, *The Book of Thel, The Marriage of Heaven and Hell* in 1790, and, in 1791, the first book of *The French Revolution:a Poem in Seven Books*, which Gilchrist says was published anonymously, in ordinary type, and without illustrations, by the bookseller Johnson. No copy of this book is known to exist[1]. At this time he was a fervent believer in the new

1. Mr. John Sampson includes in his selection of *The Poetical Works of William Blake*, 1913, the unpublished *French Revolution*. He says in his Bibliographical Introduction:

'In 1791 the bookseller Johnson set up in type with a view to publication Blake's *French Revolution*, Book I, a work known to us from a single copy only, and here reprinted for the first time. This copy, since lost sight of for half a century, would appear to have been seen by Gilchrist, Swinburne and the Rossettis, who quote the title page though no part of the contents. A transcript, partial or complete, made by Palmer about the same time for the Gilchrists, also disappeared, while, as stated in my previous edition, the late Mr. John Linnell, who had been credited with the possession of the original, disclaimed any knowledge of the book. This, however, would seem to have been an oversight, as after the death of Mr. Linnell this work was rediscovered in the family collection, and with great generosity placed at my service by Mr. Herbert Linnell. The book is a demy quarto of eighteen pages, 11 × 8 inches, printed in ordinary typography. The first quire of two leaves contains the title page and the "Advertisement" (both with verso blank), followed by two quires, B and C, in fours, paginated at head 1—16 within square brackets. The title page runs: THE FRENCH REVOLUTION. A Poem, in Seven Books. Book the First. London: Printed for J. Johnson No. 72, St. Paul's Church-yard. MDCCXCI. (Price One Shilling.) At the left-hand top corner, in pale black ink, is the inscription, not reproduced in our facsimile "John Linnell. Red Hill, 1860," the ascription "By Wm. Blake" between the third and fourth lines of the title being also in the autograph of the original owner. The poem begins on P. (I) with the dropped heading THE FRENCH REVOLUTION (line). BOOK THE FIRST (line), and concludes on p. 16, the *explicit* reading "END OF THE FIRST BOOK."

'There are strong reasons for concluding that though prepared for the press this book was never actually printed off or published. In the first

age which was to be brought about by the French Revolution, and he was much in the company of revolutionaries and freethinkers, and the only one among them who dared wear the 'bonnet rouge' in the street. Some of these, Thomas Paine, Godwin, Holcroft, and others, he met at Johnson's shop in St. Paul's Churchyard, where Fuseli and Mary Wollstonecraft also came. It was at Johnson's, in 1792, that Blake saved the life of Paine, by hurrying him off to France, with the warning, 'You must not go home, or you are a dead man,' at the very moment when a warrant had been issued for his arrest. Johnson himself was in 1798 put into gaol for his

---

place it is demonstrable that this, the only known copy, was not one of a number issued in any edition however small, but was merely a page-proof of a work which never saw the light of day, preserved, perhaps, by Blake in lieu of the original MS. This proof, though "perfected," i.e. printed on both sides, reveals a defective register showing that the formes were not made finally ready for printing. Farther evidence of this being a proof only is found in the "excessive impression" or heavy pull of the press almost cutting through the thin paper, in the tell-tale thumb-mark of the printer, the grey and uneven colouring and blurriness at ends of lines, the fact that the final line "End of the First Book" is out of centre, and other typographical details. The text, though set with fair accuracy and punctuated to the best of the printer's ability, has more than one misprint which could hardly have escaped the eye of the proofreader: e.g. "Eeternally" at the beginning of line 15 of p. 3 "were away" for "wear away" on p. 5, line 5, and an inverted 8 in the page number etc. Lastly the sheets are not stitched through the centre of the quires as in an ordinary pamphlet, but are fastened to the pale-blue paper which forms the cover in Blake's usual rude mode of binding by a fine cord laced through three punctured holes.

'An advertisement on the recto of A2 states that "The remaining Books are finished, and will be published in their order," and if this statement is to be accepted literally these books would seem to be irretrievably lost. The period dealt with in the First Book, treated of course imaginatively rather than historically, describes the Convocation of the Notables before the summoning of the States General and the fall of the Bastille. Probably this First Book was written in the same year, 1789, and, as I have elsewhere conjectured, submitted to the publisher together with *Tiriel*. The fact that the compositors' labours occupied a year or two is in accordance with Johnson's reputation as a slow and dilatory printer. We have no knowledge of the reason which interfered with the regular publication of this work; but it can scarcely have been a rupture with his friend the bookseller, for whom Blake continued to engrave during several years, and who acted as his co-publisher in *For Children: The Gates of Paradise* in 1793. Possibly Johnson, who, in spite of his revolutionary sympathies, had in 1791 declined to publish Paine's *Rights of Man*, might have thought it prudent not to proceed further with Blake's work, or the latter, feeling that the book would be out of date before it appeared, may himself have withdrawn it prior to publication.'

republican sympathies, and continued to give his weekly literary dinners in gaol.

Blake's back-windows at Poland Street looked out on the yard of Astley's circus, and Tatham tells a story of Blake's wonder, indignation, and prompt action on seeing a wretched youth chained by the foot to a horse's hobble. The neighbour whom he regarded as 'hired to depress art,' Sir Joshua Reynolds, died in 1792. A friend quoted by Gilchrist tells us: 'When a very young man he had called on Reynolds to show him some designs, and had been recommended to work with less extravagance and more simplicity, and to correct his drawing. This Blake seemed to regard as an affront never to be forgotten. He was very indignant when he spoke of it.' There is also a story of a meeting between Blake and Reynolds, when each, to his own surprise, seems to have found the other very pleasant.

Blake's mother died in 1792, at the age of seventy, and was buried in Bunhill Fields on September 9. In the following year he moved to 13 Hercules Buildings, Lambeth,[1] where, during the next seven years, he did engraving, both of his own designs and of those of others, and published the engraved book of designs called *The Gates of Paradise* (1793), the poems and illustrations of the *Songs of Experience* (1794), and the greater part of the Prophetic Books, besides writing, apparently in 1797, the vast and never really finished MS. of *The Four Zoas*. This period was that of which we have the largest and most varied result, in written and engraved work, together with a large number of designs, including five hundred and thirty-seven done on the margin of Young's *Night Thoughts*, and the earliest of the colour prints. This was Blake's one period of something like prosperity, as we gather from several stories reported by Tatham, who says that during

1. Gilchrist (i. p. 98) gives a long account of the house which he took to be Blake's, and which he supposed to be on the west side of Hercules Road. But it has been ascertained beyond a doubt, on the authority of the Lambeth rate-books, confirmed by Norwood's map of London at the end of the eighteenth century, that Blake's house, then numbered 13 Hercules Buildings, was on the east side of the road, and is the house now numbered 23 Hercules Road. Before 1842 the whole road was renumbered, starting at the south end of the western side and returning by the eastern side, so that the house which Gilchrist saw in 1863 as 13 Hercules Buildings was what afterwards became 70 Hercules Road, and is now pulled down.The road was finally renumbered in 1890, and the house became 23 Hercules Road.

the absence of Blake and his wife on one of their long country walks, which would take up a whole day, thieves broke into the house, and 'carried away plate to the value of £60 and clothes to the amount of £40 more.' Another £40 was lent by Blake to 'a certain freethinking speculator, the author of many elaborate philosophical treatises,' who complained that 'his children had not a dinner.' A few days afterwards the Blakes went to see the destitute family, and the wife 'had the audacity to ask Mrs. Blake's opinion of a very gorgeous dress, purchased the day following Blake's compassionate gift.' Yet another story is of a young art-student who used to pass the house every day carrying a portfolio under his arm, and whom Blake pitied for his poverty and sickly looks, and taught for nothing and looked after till he died. Blake had other pupils too, among 'families of high rank,' but being 'aghast' at the prospect of 'an appointment to teach drawing to the Royal Family,' he gave up all his pupils, with his invariably exquisite sense of manners, on refusing the royal offer.

It was in 1799 that Blake found his first patron, and one of his best friends, in Thomas Butts, 'that remarkable man—that great patron of British genius,' as Samuel Palmer calls him, who, for nearly thirty years, with but few intervals, continued to buy whatever Blake liked to do for him, paying him a small but steady price, and taking at times a drawing a week. A story which, as Palmer says, had 'grown in the memory,' connects him with Blake at this time, and may be once more repeated, if only to be discredited. There was a back-garden at the house in Hercules Buildings, and there were vines in it, which Blake would never allow to be pruned, so that they grew luxuriant in leaf and small and harsh in fruit. Mr. Butts, according to Gilchrist, is supposed to have come one day into 'Blake's Arcadian Arbour,' as Tatham calls it, and to have found Blake and his wife sitting naked, reading out Milton's *Paradise Lost* 'in character,' and to have been greeted with: 'Come in, it is only Adam and Eve.' John Linnell, in some notes written after reading Gilchrist, and quoted in Story's *Life of Linnell*, writes with reason: 'I do not think it possible. Blake was very unreserved in his narrations to me of all his thoughts and actions, and I think if anything like this story had been true, he would have told me of it. I am sure he would have laughed heartily at it if it had been told of him or of anybody else, for he was a hearty laugher at absurdities.' In such a matter, Linnell's authority may' well be final, if indeed any authority is required, beyond a sense of humour, and the knowledge that Blake possessed it.

Another legend of the period, which has at least more significance, whether true or not, is referred to by both Swinburne and Mr. W. M. Rossetti, on what authority I cannot discover, and is thus stated by Messrs. Ellis and Yeats: 'It is said that Blake wished to add a concubine to his establishment in the Old Testament manner, but gave up the project because it made Mrs. Blake cry.' 'The element of fable,' they add, 'lies in the implication that the woman who was to have wrecked this household had a bodily existence.... There is a possibility that he entertained mentally some polygamous project, and justified it on some patriarchal theory. A project and theory are one thing, however, and a woman is another; and though there is abundant suggestion of the project and theory, there is no evidence at all of the woman.' I have found in the unpublished part of Crabb Robinson's *Diary* and *Reminiscences* more than a 'possibility' or even 'abundant suggestion' that Blake accepted the theory as a theory. Crabb Robinson himself was so frightened by it that he had to confide it to his *Diary* in the disguise of German, though, when he came to compile his *Reminiscences* many years later he ventured to put it down in plain English which no editor has yet ventured to print. Both passages will be found in their place in the verbatim reprint given later; but I will quote the second here:

'13*th June* (1826).—I saw him again in June. He was as wild as ever, says my journal, but he was led to-day to make assertions more palpably mischievous and capable of influencing other minds, and immoral, supposing them to express the will of a responsible agent, than anything he had said before. As for instance, that he had learned from the Bible that wives should be in common. And when I objected that Marriage was a Divine institution he referred to the Bible, "that from the beginning it was not so." He affirmed that he had committed many murders, and repeated his doctrine, that reason is the only Sin, and that careless, gay people are better than those who think, etc., etc.'

This passage leaves no doubt as to Blake's theoretical view of marriage, but it brings us no nearer to any certainty as to his practical action in the matter. With Blake, as with all wise men, a mental decision in the abstract had no necessary influence on conduct. To have the courage of your opinions is one thing, and

Blake always had this; but he was of all people least impelled to go and do a thing because he considered the thing a permissible one to do. Throughout all his work Blake affirms freedom as the first law of love; jealousy is to him the great iniquity, the unforgivable selfishness. He has the frank courage to praise in *The Visions of the Daughters of Albion*:

'Infancy, fearless, lustful, happy, nestling for delight
In laps of pleasure! Innocence, honest, open, seeking
The vigorous joys of morning light';

and of woman he asks, 'Who taught thee modesty, subtle modesty?' In the same book, which is Blake's Book of Love, Oothoon offers 'girls of mild silver or of furious gold' to her lover; in the paradisal state of '*Jerusalem* 'every female delights to give her maiden to her husband.' All these things are no doubt symbols, but they are symbols which meet us on every page of Blake, and I do not doubt that to him they represented an absolute truth. Therefore I think it perfectly possible that some 'mentally polygamous project' was at one time or another entertained by him, and 'justified on some patriarchal theory.' What I am sure of, however, is that a tear of Mrs. Blake ('for a tear is an intellectual thing') was enough to wipe out project if not theory, and that one to whom love was pity more than it was desire would have given no nearer cause for jealousy than some unmortal Oothoon.

It was in 1794 that Blake engraved the *Songs of Experience*. Four of the Prophetic Books had preceded it, but here Blake returns to the clear and simple form of the *Songs of Innocence*, deepening it with meaning and heightening it with ardour. Along with this fierier art the symbolic contents of what, in the *Songs of Innocence*, had been hardly more than a child's strayings in earthly or divine Edens, becomes angelic, and speaks with more deliberately hid or doubled meanings. Even 'The Tiger,' by which Lamb was to know that here was 'one of the most extraordinary persons of the age,' is not only a sublime song about a flame-like beast, but contains some hint that 'the tigers of wrath are wiser than the horses of instruction.' In this book, and in the poems which shortly followed it, in that MS. book whose contents have sometimes been labelled, after a rejected title of Blake's, *Ideas of Good and Evil*, we see Blake more wholly and more evenly himself than anywhere else in his work. From these central poems we can distinguish the complete type of Blake as a poet.

Blake is the only poet who sees all temporal things under the form of eternity. To him reality is merely a symbol, and he catches at its terms, hastily and faultily, as he catches at the lines of the drawing-master, to represent, as in a faint image, the clear and shining outlines of what he sees with the imagination; through the eye, not with it, as he says. Where other poets use reality as a springboard into space, he uses it as a foothold on his return from flight. Even Wordsworth seemed to him a kind of atheist, who mistook the changing signs of 'vegetable nature' for the unchanging realities of the imagination. 'Natural objects,' he wrote in a copy of Wordsworth, 'always did and now do weaken, deaden, and obliterate imagination in me. Wordsworth must know that what he writes valuable is not to be found in nature.' And so his poetry is the most abstract of all poetry, although in a sense the most concrete. It is everywhere an affirmation, the register of vision; never observation. To him observation was one of the daughters of memory, and he had no use for her among his Muses, which were all eternal, and the children of the imagination. 'Imagination.' he said, 'has nothing to do with memory.' For the most part he is just conscious that what he Sees as 'an old man grey' is no more than a 'frowning thistle':

> 'For double the vision my eyes do see,
> And a double vision is always with me.
> With my inward eyes, 'tis an old man grey,
> With my outward, a thistle across my way.'

In being so far conscious, he is only recognizing the symbol, not admitting the reality.

In his earlier work, the symbol still interests him, he accepts it without dispute; with, indeed, a kind of transfiguring love. Thus he writes of the lamb and the tiger, of the joy and sorrow of infants, of the fly and the lily, as no poet of mere observation has ever written of them, going deeper into their essence than Wordsworth ever went into the heart of daffodils, or Shelley into the nerves of the sensitive plant. He takes only the simplest flowers or weeds, and the most innocent or most destroying of animals, and he uses them as illustrations of the divine attributes. From the same flower and beast he can read contrary lessons without change of meaning, by the mere transposition of qualities, as in the poem which now reads:

'The modest rose puts forth a thorn,
The humble sheep a threatening horn;
While the lily white shall in love delight,
Nor a thorn, nor a threat, stain her beauty bright.'

I have just said, 'Which now reads,' and for this definitive version we are indebted to Mr. Sampson, whose edition of Blake is a masterpiece of editing; for Blake, of all modern English poets, was most in need of a good editor. The text of Blake, as it can be read in the two most accessible editions — W. M. Rossetti's in the 'Aldine' series, and Yeats's in 'The Muses' Library' — differs widely, and in neither edition does it even profess to be printed as Blake wrote it. It is to D. G. Rossetti that we owe the recovery, if not almost the discovery, of Blake; it-is to Swinburne that we owe the most generous and penetrating study of his work that has yet been made. Yet it is to Rossetti, and in a minor degree to Swinburne, that we owe that adulteration of the original text which has left it, as Mr. Sampson truly says, 'a sort of poor palimpsest where each new owner has overwritten his own poetry.' The text of Yeats is more faithful than that of Rossetti, but it rearranges the material with much freedom, omits and emends many poems, and contains numerous inaccuracies. 'It will be seen,' says Mr. Sampson, referring to the various editions, 'that scarcely a single poem or even epigram has been suffered to remain as Blake wrote it'

In this new edition the text is printed verbatim from the' manuscript, engraved, and letterpress originals; 'Blake's final version is uniformly adopted as the text, while all earlier or cancelled readings are supplied in footnotes. All the poems are arranged exactly as they are found, and each group is given, as far as is known, in chronological order. The two main MS. sources, the Rossetti and the Pickering MSS., are now printed for the first time from careful and accurate transcripts, made by the present owner, Mr. W.A. White, of Brooklyn, New York, whose generous and scrupulous labour deserves grateful recognition from every student of Blake. Each section has a comprehensive and minute bibliographical introduction; the greater part of the poems, in addition to the variorum readings, have footnotes explaining, completing, or interpreting the text in many cases showing Blake at work on his material, stage by stage; and there is a condensed, but excellent *catalogue raisonné* of the Prophetic Books. Many dates are now fixed for the first time; a few fragments are for the first time printed; in short it is now possible to read the whole of Blake's poems exactly as he wrote them.

On one of the pages in which Messrs. Ellis and Yeats make the unjustifiable statement that

'if the present version had been read aloud to Blake within twenty-four hours of the composition of his own piece, he would not have known that he had not written what is here printed,'

they add:

'But if the best of originators, he was the poorest of correctors, most of all in cases where his lines may really be said to correct themselves.'

It has been the error of all Blake's editors to think this, and to act on their theory that Blake's lines 'correct themselves.' Mr. Sampson proves by his edition, in which only Blake's own corrections of his lines are supplied, that Blake was as great a corrector as he was an originator. In but one or two instances did Blake prefer finally an obviously inferior reading, while his improvements are visible on almost every page to anyone who goes carefully through the variorum readings. Here and there, of course, are slips of grammar and jolts of metre; but even when these have been rectified 'by the best of emendators something – and something characteristic of Blake – is almost invariably lost. Take, for instance, the beautiful early lines 'To the Evening Star,' which are written in a form of blank verse whose very incorrectnesses foreshadow that later measure of the Prophetic Books in which Blake professes to have 'produced a variety in every line, both of cadences and number of syllables.' The germs of this later style are clearly visible in such lines as:

'Smile on our loves, and whilst thou drawest the
Blue curtains of the sky, scatter thy silver dew
On every flower that shuts its sweet eyes
In timely sleep.'

That is how they are printed, but in Rossetti's version they read:

'whilst thou drawest round
The curtains of the sky, scatter thy dew';

and in Swinburne's:

'while thou drawest round,
The sky's blue curtains, scatter silver dew,

Both also alter 'shuts' to 'closes.' The two versions are extremely characteristic—of Rossetti and of Swinburne, whose *facture* of verse might almost be divined from them; but they have cease to be characteristic of the Blake of 1783, and they no longer help to explain the Blake of 1793.

The chief instance of a poem permanently spoilt by Blake, and thus necessarily represented in Mr. Sampson's text by an inferior reading, is the poem generally known as 'Love's Secret,' which begins 'Never seek to tell thy love.' Blake omitted the beautiful first stanza, and altered the lovely ending, 'He took her with a sigh,' into the harsh and grotesque 'O! was no deny.' Mr. Sampson, of course, gives the earlier readings in his footnotes, but this is an instance in which he would have done well to print both versions in full, as he has done in several other not more important instances. Two pages later there is a fine example of those generally wise changes which are now seen for the first time in the text: the change of 'And 'twixt earnest and joke' to the more concrete, less didactic, certainly more imaginative 'And still as a maid,' in the poem beginning.

'I asked a thief to steal me a peach.'

On p. 198 a lovely new reading has been recaptured in the poem called 'Morning,' which has always been printed:

'Sweet morning leads me on;
With soft repentant moan
I see the break of day.'

What Blake really wrote was:

'Sweet mercy leads me on
With soft repentant moan;
I see the break of day.'

The most important of the new readings, however, is the final text of the poem, first called 'In a Myrtle Shade.'This, originally sixteen lines in length, was altered and cut down again and again, and these different versions are given inaccurately in the edition of Yeats, who prints as Blake's final text a version which ends with two lines omitted by Blake. The final version, as given by Mr. Sampson, is reduced from sixteen to six lines, and has attained perfection.

The pages of Mr. Sampson's edition from 178 to 182 will repay careful study. There we see Blake for once unable to extricate himself from the tangle of his own twisting, attempting again and again to mould the substance and straighten the form of what had never been wholly mastered by his imagination. Not even the five pages which give us the whole process of gestation of what came at last to be the masterpiece of 'The Tiger' are more significant in their revelation of Blake's manner of work. In the first version of 'The Fly,' whose 'tiny metre' seems as if it must have been twin-born with its thought, we find Blake beginning in a heavy metre, thus:

'Woe! alas! my guilty hand
Brushed across thy summer joy:
All thy gilded painted pride
Shattered, fled...'

The four lines called 'The Lily,' now so placid a song of innocence, are seen in one of the most interesting of the notes to have been begun in exactly the opposite mood:

'Beginning by writing:

"The rose puts envious.."

he felt that "envious" did not express his full meaning, and deleted the last three words, writing above them "lustful rose," and finishing the line with the words "puts forth a thorn." He then went on:

"The coward sheep a threat'ning horn;
While the lilly white shall in love delight,
And the lion increase freedom and peace,"

at which point he drew a line under the poem to show it was finished. On a subsequent reading he deleted the last line, substituting for it:

"The priest loves war, and the soldier peace.'

but here, perceiving that his rime had disappeared, he cancelled this line also, and gave the poem an entirely different turn by changing the word "lustful" to "modest" and "coward" to "humble," and completing the quatrain (as in the engraved version) by a fourth line simply explanatory of the first three.'

In more than one poem we find Blake, after he had written it, realizing that, though it was clear to his own mind, it would be to the reader no more than a lock without a key, and promptly supplying the key in the form of an introductory stanza, as in 'The Wild Flower's Song' (p. 170). Throughout, indeed, we are able to realize, and for the first time, the sane and alert critical quality which accompanied or followed Blake in what have seemed to many his almost unconscious improvisations.

When I say that Blake reads lessons, let it not be supposed that he was ever consciously didactic. Conduct does not concern him; not doing, but being. He held that education was the setting of a veil between light and the soul. 'There is no good in education,' he said. 'I hold it to be wrong. It is the great sin. It is eating of the tree of the knowledge of good and evil. This was the fault of Plato. He knew nothing but the virtues and vices and good and evil. There is nothing in all that. Everything is good in God's eyes.' And, as he says with his excellent courage: 'When I tell the truth, it is not for the sake of convincing those who do not know it, but for the sake of defending those who do'; and, again, with still more excellent and harder courage: 'When I am endeavouring to think rightly, I must not regard my own any more than other people's weaknesses'; so, in his poetry, there is no moral tendency, nothing that might not be poison as well as antidote; nothing, indeed, but the absolute affirmation of that energy which is eternal delight. He worshipped energy as the well-head or parent fire of life; and to him there was no evil, only a weakness, a negation of energy, the ignominy of wings that droop and are contented in the dust.

And so, like Nietzsche, but with a deeper innocence, he finds himself 'beyond good and evil,' in a region where the soul is naked and its own master. Most of his art is the unclothing of the soul, and when at last it is naked and alone, in that 'thrilling' region where the souls of other men have at times penetrated, only to shudder back with terror from the brink of eternal loneliness, then only is this soul exultant with the supreme happiness.

Of the books on William Blake to be noted at this point, Mr. Ellis calls his *The Real Blake,* and he gives us an immense amount of information, heaped in bewildering fashion, and ticketed with labels and comments which can hardly fail to increase that bewilderment. His enthusiasm is boundless; he is intimately acquainted with everything that Blake wrote, and everything that has been written about Blake. His belief is that he has discovered the meaning of Blake's philosophy in every detail, and that this meaning can be made mathematically evident. He sets himself to correct every error which he finds in Blake's metre, and to interpret every significance which he distinguishes in Blake's acts and words. He pours out in one ceaseless stream information, speculation, controversy; and his opinions are as positive as his facts are uncertain. He will put *sic* against his own misprint, and condemn Gilchrist for a slight error while he is in the very act of making it worse. He attacks other writers on Blake for pedantry, yet what is it but a form of pedantry to accumulate irrelevant corrections of often imaginary errors? He condemns Dr. Garnet with great vehemence for opinions which he is fully justified in not sharing, but which do no more than indicate temperamental flaws in a writer who was always scrupulously anxious to be just. He returns needlessly to a fixed idea that Swinburne, who has done more than anyone else to give Blake his due place in English literature, 'pretended to like' Blake's poetry', but 'could not understand it.' And, in his desire to explain everything to the meanest capacity, he does not see that, while Blake is often difficult, his own explanation of Blake is more difficult. He has written his whole book as an explanation, and our complaint is that he explains where only a statement is wanted, and that by the time the explanation is half over the statement is more than half obscured. The intention is that no fine shade should be suffered to escape; the result is a 'blotting and blurring' of outlines in themselves 'hard and determinate' enough, after the manner of Blake's most 'outrageous demons.'

In his preoccupation with one side of Blake's work, Mr. Ellis gives us no adequate representation of Blake either as poet or painter. Details he offers, but no fine criticism—not a word which shows that he has any true knowledge of what was best in Blake's work in both arts. He goes out of his way to upset the foolish legends or theories which have been invented, but he supplies their place with suggestions not less chimerical, interpretations not less futile. His attitude is too often that of prying curiosity, and he expatiates for pages on discreditable stories which have no foundation, and which, he tells us a hundred pages farther on, he does not himself believe. Here is a specimen of what we have called explanation in the place of statement. Tatham tells us that Blake said to the woman whom he was afterwards to marry: 'Do you pity me? Then I love you.' This might be thought to be sufficiently explicit. But Mr. Ellis, after quibbling as to exactly what Blake said and exactly what emphasis he laid on this or that word, continues:

'Whichever way the expression is read it means: "I, who have so lately loved, have already seen that you love me; and you are so pretty and dear that I have been sorry to think that I could not love you for such qualities—Polly Woods was pretty and dear—and I have often wished that I could find something different to love you for. I find it now in your pity." '

Does this bring us any nearer to the 'real Blake'?

Some of the material is valuable: a very interesting letter to Cumberland is printed for the first time; and the important marginalia to Reynolds, Swedenborg and Lavater are given more fully, and in a more convenient form, than in Gilchrist or the Quaritch edition. But how much their value is diminished by the careless copying or printing, which has filled them with errors! The *Public Address* and the fragmentary descriptions of the picture of the *Last Judgment*, reprinted from the Quaritch edition, retain the same misprints, and even a reference to 'the chapter on the MS. Book, Vol. I., p. 332,' which refers (not even accurately, for the page is 232) to that edition, although the passage in question is reprinted on p. 432 of *The Real Blake*. The fact of one or two slight additions having been made seems to indicate that Blake's MS. has been again consulted, yet the text as it stands has evidently not been corrected from it. The *Descriptive Catalogue* is somewhat needlessly given, as it is accessible in Gilchrist, and it follows Gilchrist's errors, or arbitrary changes. *An Island in the Moon* 'is printed for the first time in full, and to print it at all is to do a disservice to Blake, for it has no value apart from some of the songs, which have often been reprinted. In a passage near the end which has often been quoted Mr. Ellis leaves out half of one of the sentences.

It is regrettable that, concerning Mr. Sampson's book, Mr. Ellis should assure us it is 'empty of interpretation or intelligent poetic study.' This may be reasonably denied; it may be fairly said that no other edition contains anything like the same amount of material for study and interpretation. But the main point is this—that Mr. Sampson gives, as nearly as he could, the exact text which Blake wrote; and that is all that anyone (whether or not a 'mere pedant,' as Mr. Ellis puts it) wants to read in an edition of Blake. Mr. Ellis expressly says that he has given, not what Blake wrote, but what he 'thought he had written'; or, in other words, what Mr. Ellis thought Blake ought to have written.

But Mr. Ellis, who thinks he knows what Blake ought to have written, cannot come to any final conclusion as to what that really was, and gives a new version every time he reprints his text. In *The Real Blake* he devotes several pages to explaining how Blake meant to write the opening lines of the fragment of *Edward III*. One of the lines reads

'The enemy fight in chains, invisible chains, but heavy.'

In his edition of the poems Mr. Ellis prints this line:

'The enemy fight in chains, invisible, heavy.'

But in *The Real Blake* he alters it again into

'The enemy fight in chains, unseen but heavy,'

which we find is a return to the text of his Quaritch edition of 1893.

Another line, originally printed

'When confusion rages, when the field is in a flame,'

which Mr. Ellis printed in 1893

'When on the fields in flame, confusion rages,

and in 1906

'When confusion rages, when the field's in flame,'

he now suggests printing as

'When confusion rages,—when the field's aflame,'—

and he evidently supposes that he has brought a radical change of metre into the line as Blake left it—that he has corrected it, in short. As a matter of fact, he has left it, metrically, exactly where it was.

Mr. Ellis has an unfortunate theory that Blake was unable to revise his own work, and that even when he altered it he was as likely as not to alter it for the worse. 'There were two Blakes, and they could not edit one another. Yet he absolutely requires editing. Now the fact is that although Blake, like every poet who could write swiftly, has left here and there an obvious slip of the pen, he was for the most part a careful writer, and an almost invariably successful reviser. We have only to study Mr. Sampson's variorum edition to see how subtly Blake worked on his own text, and how finally (as in the lines 'To my Myrtle') he could extricate form and idea alike from the tangle out of which they had grown. To say that Blake 'did not because he could not' correct his own work, and that to leave him uncorrected is 'the very cowardice of pedantry,' is therefore unfair.

Mr. Ellis invents in these pages minute circumstances in Blake's life for which there is not the slightest evidence, and fills pages with still more minute analysis of the probable effect on Blake of these circumstances. The early chapter called 'Mary' is made up from a poem of that name, the date of which he assumes to be 1783 or 1784; and it is on this date that he has spun the whole web of indiscreet speculation. Now according to Mr. Sampson's clear reasoning there is little doubt that the poem was written between 1801 and 1803. If this is the case, the web has nothing to hang by. And, to put aside the question of date, there is not in the poem, nor in any known source of information, any suggestion of the circumstances which Mr. Ellis gives in a way to lead the reader to suppose that they are founded on fact. He actually invents the legend of an unborn child, of how 'Catherine was at that moment on her way to become a mother.' Having spent nearly seven pages in telling this imaginary story as if it were a fact, he suddenly adds that 'Mary'is 'not merely Blake's wife, but the lyrical and emotional side of his genius, and he is not *merely* writing about Catherine but also about this part of his own nature.'

And a page farther on he admits:

'"Mary" *might*, therefore, have been only an aspect of his own mind.

It is this juggling with facts and fancies that makes so much of this copious and enthusiastic book unsatisfactory. It is written to do honour to Blake and to explain him, but it requires both correction and explanation before it can do either.

Swinburne's critical essay' on Blake was published in 1868, just after the 'discovery' of Blake in Gilchrist's *Life*, and some eight years before the publication of any collected edition of the poems. Yet, notwithstanding certain new facts which have seen gathered, notwithstanding the better order into which he existing material has been put, notwithstanding the valuable Interpretative work of Mr. Yeats in his *Ideas of Good and Evil,* it can fairly be said that nothing in Swinburne's book (except a few facts and dates, unimportant in themselves) has been really superseded. Not a word in the text is altered.To reprint a book of criticism after forty Years without the alteration of a word as something heroic in it which suits a critic whose criticism has always been one form of his poetry, or more rightly its overflow.

The motto from Baudelaire, saying how inevitably a perfect poet turns at one moment or another to that self-examination which in a poet is the criticism of poetry, applies to no one better than to Swinburne. Swinburne is a critic because he is a poet, and for no other reason. This book on Blake is the best of his books of criticism, because in it he is more wholly content to be a poet than in any other. In what he has written of Blake, a poet divines a poet; and no error in such a divination can be essential. Much of what seemed to Blake vital seems to Swinburne mere 'fever and fancy'. He is needlessly petulant towards 'some Hibernian commentator on Blake, if I rightly remember a fact so insignificant' (if this is meant forYeats, should not Ellis have his share in the mockery?), because, we suppose, these gentlemen, in the preface to their book, said that 'not one clear paragraph about the myth of Four Zoas is to be found in all' that Swinburne, in common with Gilchrist and the two Rossettis, had published. Well, Swinburne has not fully elucidated the Four Zoas, nor has he tried very hard to do so, because that is not the part of poetry or of imagination which interests him. Perhaps the Four Zoas could be made clear, or even coherent; but in the book of Ellis and Yeats they certainly become more obscure as some mechanical coherence seems to come into them. Swinburne, it is evident throughout his book, is personally exasperated by the whole 'system' or 'mythology'; yet, in spite of this, he has set himself with an amazing patience to unravel just so much of the meaning of these crabbed prophecies as is needed to be able to follow the main lines of their beauty as poems. This he has done; more than this he has not tried or professed to do.

Where Swinburne's book is invaluable is in his interpretation of poetry as poetry, of symbolism as poetry, of pictorial design as poetry. It is difficult to imagine that Swinburne really cares for music, or painting, or any form of art outside poetry. He absorbs every form of art, and they all turn to poetry, and can be rendered by him only in terms of poetry. In this huge book of criticism, in which the main incidents of the life of Blake are told, and a detailed account is given of nearly the whole of his literary and much of his painted and engraved work, there is not a page—not even in those flaming footnotes which spire from page to page after the dwindling body of the text—which is not essentially poetry rather than prose. The eloquence and the instinct are alike those of the poet, and these lamenting and triumphing sentences through which Blake speaks again, as through the mouth of a herald, must be read as a new creation of beauty, an affirmation rather than a criticism. No poet has ever put so much of the substance, and whatever is translatable of the form, of poetry into prose. And the consequence is that the prose is often defined as extravagant, and the criticism as unbalanced. It has the balance of an arrow in flight: it hits the mark.

Swinburne is a great praiser, and to praise the right things with due energy is the highest privilege of the critic. He is perhaps the only critic of our time who has never, by design or accident, praised the wrong things. His extraordinary catholicity, his complete lack of even the prejudice natural to poets,' is sufficiently proved by a single clause in his prefatory note to this new edition. He speaks of Blake as 'the greatest English poet except Collins who had the fortune or misfortune to be born into a century far greater in progress than in poetry.' That little clause 'except Collins,' though we need not take it to mean more than it says—besides Collins, not next to Collins—gives its author the right to say all that he says in the rest of the book about Blake. The really extravagant, the really unbalanced critic, is equally the critic who can accept Collins and not Blake, or he who can accept Blake and not Collins. And if Swinburne has seemed to praise to excess, say, the poorest work ot Victor Hugo, how little it matters when one remembers what the best work is like! And let us not be too hasty in saying that any recent work has been praised to excess. What it seemed extravagant to say about Blake in 1866 is like a twice—told tale in 1906. So time follows the seer.

The main quality in Swinburne's criticism is its exultation. 'There is a joy in praising' might have been written for him, and he communicates to us, as few writers do, his own sense of joy in beauty. No doubt it would be possible to be very much annoyed by many of the things—and as many in this as in any other of his books—that Swinburne has said, not only about literature, but also about religion and morals and politics. But he has never said anything on any of these subjects which is not generous, and high-minded, and, at least for the moment, passionately sincere."If I contradict myself, I contradict myself," has been said by a poet about whom Swinburne has said many mutually contradictory things, all true in their way. The fine praise of Walt Whitman and the ingenious comparison of him with Blake at the end of this book could not have been written by Swinburne since the day when he wrote the essay called 'Whitmania.' It can perfectly well be reprinted by him from the year 1866, because both points of view have at different times been exclusively his, and both can be reconciled with a single conception of poetry.

But, if we do not allow ourselves to be disturbed by these extremes, at either end of them—if we realize how much of solemn jocoseness has gone to the making of these unwounding darts—we shall find it curiously exhilarating to read a criticism which quickens the blood rather than stirs the intelligence, and is like a friend talking about a friend. One cannot read this book and not love Blake, it is difficult to think of another book, written by a poet on a poet, which is so generous and so illuminating. And never for a moment does Swinburne lose his hold on that thread of 'sound reason in Blake's eccentric and fitful intelligence,' his consciousness of that 'spiritual bedrock of natural righteousness and reason,' which has not always been 'adequately acknowledged or perceived.' No one has done so much to vindicate Blake's sanity of imagination as this poet who is no mystic, and who does not naturally love a mystic. Blake's mysticism can be studied elsewhere, and defended, if not explained, by others; but what Swinburne has done is to set the man of genius in his own place as a maker, a poet; he has challenged the world to accept Blake, not for his doctrine, not as either prophet or visionary, but as the writer of great poems and the artist of great designs.

CHAPTER V

It is to the seven years at Lambeth that what may be called the first period of the Prophetic Books largely belongs, though it does not indeed begin there. The roots of it are strongly visible in *The Marriage of Heaven and Hell*, which was written at Poland Street, and they may be traced even further back. Everything else, until we come to the last or Felpham period, which has a new quality of its own, belongs to Lambeth.

In his earlier work Blake is satisfied with natural symbols, with nature as symbol; in his later work, in the final message of the Prophetic Books, he is no longer satisfied with what then seems to him the relative truth of the symbols of reality. Dropping the tools with which he has worked so well, he grasps with naked hands after an absolute truth of statement, which is like his attempt in his designs to render the outlines of vision literally, without translation into the forms of human sight. He invents names harsh as triangles, Enitharmon, Theotormon, Rintrah, for spiritual states and essences, and he employs them as Wagner employed his leading motives, as a kind of shorthand for the memory. His meaning is no longer apparent in the ordinary meaning of the words he uses; we have to read him with a key, and the key is not always in our hands; he forgets that he is talking to men on the earth in some language which he has learnt in heavenly places. He sees symbol within symbol, and as he tries to make one clear to us, he does but translate it into another, perhaps no easier, or more confusing. And it must be remembered, when even interpreters like Mr. Ellis and Mr. Yeats falter, and confess 'There is apparently some confusion among the symbols,' that after all we have only a portion of Blake's later work, and that probably a far larger portion was destroyed when the Peckham 'angel,' Mr. Tatham (co-partner in foolish wickedness with War-burton's cook), sat down to burn the books which he did not understand. Blake's great system of wheels within wheels remains no better than a ruin, and can but at the best be pieced together tentatively by those who are able to trace the connection of some of its parts. It is no longer even possible to know how much consistency Blake was able to give to his symbols, and how far he failed to make them visible in terms of mortal understanding. As we have them, they evade us on every side, not because they are meaningless, but because the secret of their meaning is so closely kept. To Blake actual contemporary names meant even more than they meant to Walt Whitman. 'All truths wait in all things,' said Walt Whitman, and Blake has his own quite significant but perplexing meaning when he writes:

'The corner of Broad Street weeps; Poland Street languishes
To Great Queen Street and Lincoln's Inn: all is distress and woe.'

He is concerned now only with his message, with the 'minutely particular' statement of it; and as he has ceased to accept any mortal medium, or to allow himself to be penetrated by the sunlight of earthly beauty, he has lost the means of making that message visible to us. It is a miscalculation of means, a contempt for possibilities; not, as people were once hasty enough to assume, the irresponsible rapture of madness. There is not even in these crabbed chronicles the wild beauty of the madman's scattering brain; there is a concealed sanity, a precise kind of truth, which, as Blake said of all truth, 'can never be so told as to be understood, and not be believed.'

Blake's form, or apparent formlessness, in the Prophetic Books, was no natural accident, or unconsidered utterance of inspiration. Addressing the public on the first plate of *Jerusalem* he says: 'When this verse was first dictated to me, I considered a monotonous cadence like that used by Milton and Shakespeare and all writers of English blank verse, derived from the bondage of rhyming, to be a necessary and indispensable part of verse. But I soon found that in the mouth of a true orator such monotony was not only awkward, but as much a bondage as rhyme itself. I have therefore produced a variety in every line, both of cadences and number of syllables. Every word and every letter is studied and put into its fit place; the terrific numbers are reserved for the terrific parts, the mild and gentle for the mild and gentle parts, and the prosaic for inferior parts; all are necessary to each other.' This desire for variety at the expense of unity is illustrated in one of Blake's marginal notes to Reynolds' *Discourses*. 'Such harmony of colouring' (as that of Titian in the Bacchus and Ariadne) 'is destructive of Art. One species of equal hue over all is the cursed thing called harmony. It is the smile of a fool.' This is a carrying to its extreme limit of the principle that 'there is no such thing as softness in art, and that everything in art is definite and minute... because vision is determinate and perfect'; and that 'colouring does not depend on where the colours are put, but on where the lights and darks are put, and all depends on form or outline, on where that is put.' The whole aim of the Prophetic Books is to arrive at a style as 'determinate and perfect' as vision, unmodified by any of the deceiving beauties of nature or of the distracting ornaments of conventional form. What is further interesting in Blake's statement is that he aimed, in the Prophetic Books, at producing the effect, not of poetry but of oratory, and it is as oratory, the oratory of the prophets, that the reader is doubtless meant to take them.

'Poetry fettered,' he adds, 'fetters the human race,' and I doubt not that he imagined, as Walt Whitman and later *vers-libristes* had imagined, that in casting off the form he had unfettered the spirit of poetry. There seems never to have been a time when Blake did not attempt to find for himself a freer expression than he thought verse could give him, for among the least mature of the *Poetical Sketches* are poems written in rhythmical prose, in imitation partly of Ossian, partly of the Bible. An early MS. called 'Tiriel', probably of hardly later date, still exists, written in a kind of metre of fourteen syllables, only slightly irregular in beat, but rarely fine in cadence. It already hints, in a cloudy way, at some obscure mythology, into which there already come incoherent names, of an Eastern colour, Ijim and Mnetha. Tiriel appears again in *The Book of Urizen* as Urizen's first-born, Thiriel, 'like a man from a cloud born.' Har and Heva reappear in *The Song of Los*. *The Book of Thel*, engraved in 1789, the year of the *Songs of Innocence*, is in the same metre of fourteen syllables, but written with a faint and lovely monotony of cadence, strangely fluid and flexible in that age of strong cæsuras, as in:

'Come forth, worm of the silent valley, to thy pensive queen.'

The sentiment is akin to that of the *Songs of Innocence*, and hardly more than a shadow of the mythology remains. It sings or teaches the holiness and eternity of life in all things, the equality of life in the flower, the cloud, the worm, and the maternal clay of the grave; and it ends with the unanswered question of death to life: why? why? In 1790 Blake engraved in two forms, on six and ten infinitesimal plates, a tractate which he called, There is no Natural Religion. They contain, the one commenting on the other, a clear and concise statement of many of Blake's fundamental beliefs; such as: 'That the poetic Genius is the true Man, and that the Body or outward form of Man is derived from the Poetic Genius.' 'As all men are alike in outward form, so (and with the same infinite variety) all are alike in the Poetic Genius.' 'Man's perceptions are not bounded by organs of perception, he perceives more than sense (though ever so acute) can discover.' Yet, since 'Man's desires are limited by his perceptions, none can desire what he has not perceived.' 'Therefore God becomes as we are, that we may become as He is.'

In the same year, probably, was engraved *The Marriage of Heaven and Hell*, a prose fantasy full of splendid masculine thought, and of a diabolical or infernal humour, in which Blake, with extraordinary boldness, glorifies, parodies, and renounces at once the gospel of his first master in mysticism, 'Swedenborg, strongest of men, the Samson shorn by the Churches,' as he was to call him long afterwards, in *Milton*. Blake's attitude towards Christianity might be roughly defined by calling him a heretic of the heresy of Swedenborg. *The Marriage of Heaven and Hell* begins: 'As a new heaven is begun, and it is now thirty-three years since its advent, the Eternal Hell revives. And lo! Swedenborg is the Angel sitting on the tomb: his writings are the linen clothes folded up.' Swedenborg himself, in a prophecy that Blake must have heard in his childhood, had named 1757, the year of Blake's birth, as the first of a new dispensation, the dispensation of the spirit, and Blake's acceptance of the prophecy marks the date of his escape from the too close influence of one of whom he said, as late as 1825, 'Swedenborg was a divine teacher. Yet he was wrong in endeavouring to explain to the rational faculty what reason cannot comprehend.' And so we are warned, in *The Marriage of Heaven and Hell*, against the 'confident insolence sprouting from systematic reasoning. Thus Swedenborg boasts that what he writes is new, though it is only the contents or index of already published books.' And again: 'Any man of mechanical talents may from the writings of Paracelsus or Jacob Behmen produce ten thousand volumes of equal value with Swedenborg's, and from those of Dante or Shakespeare an infinite number. But when he has done this, let him not say that he knows better than his master, for he only holds a candle in sunshine.' With Paracelsus it is doubtful if Blake was ever more than slightly acquainted; the influence of Behmen, whom he had certainly read in William Law's translation is difficult to define, and seems to have been of the most accidental or partial kind, but Swedenborg had been a sort of second Bible to him from childhood, and the influence even of his 'systematic reasoning' remained with him as at least a sort of groundwork, or despised model; 'foundations for grand things,' as he says in the *Descriptive Catalogue*. When Swedenborg says, 'Hell is divided into societies in the same manner as heaven, and also into as many societies as heaven; for every society in heaven has a society opposite to it in hell, and this for the sake of equilibrium,' we see in this spirit of meek order a matter-of-fact suggestion for Blake's 'enormous wonders of the abysses,' in which heavens and hells change names and alternate through mutual annihilations.

The last note which Blake wrote on the margins of Swedenborg's *Wisdom of Angels* is this: 'Heaven and Hell are born together.' The edition which he annotated is that of 1788, and the marginalia, which are printed in Mr. Ellis's Real Blake, will show how attentive, as late as two years before the writing of the book which that note seems to anticipate, Blake had been to every shade of meaning in one whom he was to deny with such bitter mockery. But, even in these notes, Blake is attentive to one thing only, he is reaching after a confirmation of his own sense of a spiritual language in which man can converse with paradise and render the thoughts of angels. He comments on nothing else, he seems to read only to confirm his conviction; he is equally indifferent to Swedenborg's theology and to his concern with material things; his hells and heavens, 'uses,' and 'spiritual suns,' concern him only in so far as they help to make clearer and more precise his notion of the powers and activities of the spirit in man. To Blake, as he shows us in *Milton*, Swedenborg's worst error was not even that of 'systematic reasoning,' but that of

'Showing the Transgressors in Hell: the proud Warriors in Heaven: Heaven as a Punisher and Hell as one under Punishment.'

It is for this more than for any other error that Swedenborg's 'memorable relations' are tossed back to him as 'memorable fancies,' in a solemn parody of his own manner; that his mill and vault and cave are taken from him and used against him; and that one once conversant with his heaven, and now weary of it, 'walks among the fires of hell, delighted with the enjoyments of Genius, which to Angels look like torments and insanity.' Blake shows us the energy of virtue breaking the Ten Commandments, and declares: 'Jesus was all virtue, and acted from impulse, not from rules.' Speaking through 'the voice of the Devil,' he proclaims that 'Energy is eternal delight,' and that 'Everything that lives is holy.' And, in a last flaming paradox, still mocking the manner of the analyst of heaven and hell, he bids us: 'Note. This Angel, who is now become a Devil, is my particular friend: we often read the Bible together, in its infernal or diabolical sense, which the world shall have if they behave well. I have also the Bible of Hell, which the world shall have whether they will or no.' The Bible of Hell is no doubt the Bible of Blake's new gospel, in which contraries are equally true. We may piece it together out of many fragments, of which the first perhaps is the sentence standing by itself at the bottom of the page: 'One Law for the Lion and Ox is Oppression.'

The Marriage of Heaven and Hell is loud with 'the clangour of the Arrows of Intellect,' each of the 'Proverbs of Hell 'is a jewel of concentrated wisdom, the whole book is Blake's clearest and most vital statement of his new, his reawakened belief; it contains, as I have intimated, all Nietzsche; yet something restless, disturbed, uncouth, has come violently into this mind and art, wrenching it beyond all known limits, or setting alight in it an illuminating, devouring, and unquenchable flame. In common with Swedenborg, Blake is a mystic who enters into no tradition, such as that tradition of the Catholic Church which has a liturgy awaiting dreams. For Saint John of the Cross and for Saint Teresa the words of the vision are already there, perfectly translating ecstasy into familiar speech; they have but to look and to speak. But to Blake, as to Swedenborg, no tradition is sufficiently a matter of literal belief to be at hand with its forms; new forms have to be made, and something of the crudity of Swedenborg comes over him in his rejection of the compromise of mortal imagery.

The Marriage of Heaven and Hell may be called or not called a Prophetic Book, in the strict sense; with *The Visions of the Daughters of Albion*, engraved at Lambeth in 1793, the series perhaps more literally begins. Here the fine masculine prose of *The Marriage of Heaven and Hell* has given place to a metre vaguer than the metre of *The Book of Thel*, and to a substance from which the savour has not yet gone of the *Songs of Innocence*, in such lines as:

'The new washed lamb tinged with the village smoke, and the bright swan
By the red earth of our immortal river.'

It is Blake's book of love, and it defends the honesty of the natural passions with unslackening ardour. There is no mythology in it, beyond a name or two, easily explicable. Oothoon, the virgin joy, oppressed by laws and cruelties of restraint and jealousy, vindicates her right to the freedom of innocence and to the instincts of infancy.

'And trees and birds and beasts and men behold their eternal joy.
Arise, you little glancing wings, and sing your infant joy:
Arise, and drink your bliss, for everything that lives is holy!'

It is the gospel of *The Marriage of Heaven and Hell*, and, as that proclaimed liberty for the mind, so this, with abundant rhetoric, but with vehement conviction, proclaims liberty for the body. In form it is still clear, its eloquence and imagery are partly biblical, and have little suggestion of the manner of the later Prophetic Books.

America, written in the same year, in the same measure as *The Visions of the Daughters of Albion*, is the most vehement, wild, and whirling of all Blake's prophecies. It is a prophecy of revolution, and it takes the revolt of America against England both literally and symbolically, with names of 'Washington, Franklin, Paine and Warren, Gates, Hancock and Green,' side by side with Orc and the Angel of Albion; it preaches every form of bodily and spiritual liberty in the terms of contemporary events, Boston's Angel, London's Guardian, and the like, in the midst of cataclysms of all nature, fires and thunders temporal and eternal. The world for a time is given into the power of Orc, unrestrained desire, which is to bring freedom through revolution and the destroying of the bonds of good and evil. He is called 'Antichrist, Hater of Dignities, lover of wild rebellion, and transgressor of God's Law.' He is the Satan of *The Marriage of Heaven and Hell*, and he also proclaims:

'For everything that lives is holy, life delights in life;
Because the soul of sweet delight can never be defil'd.'

As, in that book, Blake had seen 'the fiery limbs, the flaming hair' of the son of fire 'spurning the clouds written with curses, stamping the stony law to dust', so, here, he hears the voice of Orc proclaiming:

'The fierce joy, that Urizen perverted to ten commands,
What night he led the starry hosts through the wild wilderness:
That stony law I stamp to dust: and scatter religion abroad
To the four winds as a torn book, and none shall gather the leaves.'

Liberty comes in like a flood bursting all barriers:

'The doors of marriage are open, and the Priests in rustling scales
Rush into reptile coverts, hiding from the fires of Orc,
That play around the golden roofs in wreaths of fierce desire,
Leaving the females naked and glowing with the lusts of youth.
For the female spirits of the dead pining in bonds of religion
Run from their fetters reddening, and in long-drawn arches sitting,
They feel the nerves of youth renew, and desires of ancient times,
Over their pale limbs as a vine when the tender grape appears.'

The world, in this regeneration through revolution (which seemed to Blake, no doubt, a thing close at hand, in those days when France and America seemed to be breaking down the old tyrannies), is to be no longer a world laid out by convention for the untrustworthy; and he asks:

'Who commanded this? what God? what Angel?
To keep the generous from experience till the ungenerous
Are unrestrained performers of the energies of nature,
Till pity is become a trade, and generosity a science
That men get rich by.'

For twelve years, from the American to the French revolution, 'Angels and weak men' are to govern the strong, and then Europe is to be overwhelmed by the fire that had broken out in the West, though the ancient guardians of the five senses 'slow advance to shut the five gates of their law-built houses.'

'But the gates were consumed, and their bolts and hinges melted,
And the fierce flames burnt round the heavens, and round the abode of men.'

Here the myth, though it is present throughout, is an undercurrent, and the crying of the message is what is chiefly heard. *In Europe* (1794), which is written in lines broken up into frequent but not very significant irregularities, short lines alternating with long ones, in the manner of an irregular ode, the mythology is like a net or spider's web over the whole text. Names not used elsewhere, or not in the same form, are found: Manatha—Varcyon, Thiralatha, who in *Europe* is Diralada. The whole poem is an allegory of the sleep of Nature during the eighteen hundred years of the Christian era, under bonds of narrow religions and barren moralities and tyrannous laws, and of the awakening to forgotten joy, when 'Nature felt through all her pores the enormous revelry,' and the fiery spirit of Orc, beholding the morning in the east, shot to the earth,

'And in the vineyards of red France appear'd the light of his fury.'

It is another hymn of revolution, but this time an awakening more wholly mental, with only occasional contemporary allusions like that of the judge in Westminster whose wig grows to his scalp, and who is seen 'grovelling along Great George Street through the Park gate.' 'Howlings and hissings, shrieks and groans, and voices of despair,' are heard throughout; we see thought change the infinite to a serpent:

'Then was the serpent temple formed, image of infinite. Shut up in finite revolutions, and man become an angel; Heaven a mighty circle turning; God a tyrant crown'd.' The serpent temple shadows the whole island:

'Enitharmon laugh'd in her sleep to see (O woman's triumph)
Every house a den, every man bound: the shadows are filled
With spectres, and the windows wove over with curses of iron:
Over the doors Thou shalt not: and over the chimneys Fear is written:
With bands of iron round their necks fasten'd into the walls
The citizens: in leaden gyves the inhabitants of suburbs
Walk heavy: soft and bent are the bones of villagers.'

The whole book is a lament and protest, and it ends with a call to spiritual battle. In a gay and naïve prologue, written by Blake in a copy of *Europe* in the possession of Mr. Linnell, and quoted by Ellis and Yeats, Blake tells us that he caught a fairy on a streaked tulip, and brought him home:

'As we went along
Wild flowers I gathered, and he show'd me each eternal flower.

He laughed aloud to see them whimper because they were
pluck'd,
Then hover'd round me like a cloud of incense. When I came
Into my parlour and sat down and took my pen to write,
My fairy sat upon the table and dictated *Europe*.'

The First Book of Urizen (1794) is a myth, shadowed in dark symbols, of the creation of mortal life and its severing from eternity; the birth of Time out of the void and 'self-contemplating shadow' of unimaginative Reason; the creation of the senses, each a limiting of eternity, and the closing of the tent of heavenly knowledge, so that Time and the creatures of Time behold eternity no more. We see the birth of Pity and of Desire, woman the shadow and desire the child of man. Reason despairs as it realises that life lives upon death, and the cold pity of its despair forms into a chill shadow, which follows it like a spider's web, and freezes into the net of religion, or the restraint of the activities. Under this net the senses shrink inwards, and that creation which is 'the body of our death' and our stationing in time and space is finished:

'Six days they shrank up from existence,
And on the seventh they rested
And they bless'd the seventh day, in sick hope,
And forgot their eternal life.'

Then the children of reason, now 'sons and daughters of sorrow,'

'Wept and built

Tombs in the desolate places,
And form'd laws of prudence and call'd them
The eternal laws of God.'

But Fuzon, the spirit of fire, forsook the 'pendulous earth' with those children of Urizen who would still follow him.

Here, crystallised in the form of a myth, we see many of Blake's fundamental ideas. Some of them we have seen under other forms, as statement rather than as image, in *The Marriage of Heaven and Hell* and *There is no Natural Religion*. We shall see them again, developed, elaborated, branching out into infinite side-issues, multiplying upon themselves, in the later Prophetic Books, partly as myth, partly as statement; we shall see them in many of the lyrical poems, transformed into song, but still nevervarying in their message; and we shall see them, in the polemical prose of all the remaining fragments, and in the private letters, and in the annotations of Swedenborg, and in Crabb Robinson's records of conversations. *The Book of Urizen* is a sort of nucleus, the germ of a system.

Next to *The Book of Urizen,* if we may judge from the manner of its engraving, came *The Song of Los* (1795), written in a manner of vivid declamation, the lines now lengthening, now shrinking, without fixed beat or measure. It is the song of Time, 'the Eternal Prophet,' and tells the course of inspiration as it passes from east to west, 'abstract philosophy' in Brahma, 'forms of dark delusion' to Moses on Mount Sinai, the mount of law; 'a gospel from wretched Theotormon' (distressed human love and pity) to Jesus, 'a man of sorrows'; the 'loose Bible' of Mahomet, setting free the senses; Odin's 'code of war.'

'These were the Churches, Hospitals, Castles, Palaces,
Like nets and gins and traps to catch the joys of Eternity,
And all the rest a desert:
Till like a dream Eternity was obliterated and erased.'

'The vast of Nature' shrinks up before the 'shrunken eyes' of men, till it is finally enclosed in the 'philosophy of the five senses,' the philosophy of Newton and Locke. 'The Kings of Asia,' the cruelties of the heathen, the ancient powers of evil, call on 'famine from the heath, pestilence from the fen,'

'To turn man from his path,
To restrain the child from the womb,
To cut off the bread from the city,
That the remnant may learn to obey,
That the pride of the heart may fail,
That the lust of the eyes may be quench'd,
That the delicate ear in its infancy
May be dull'd, and the nostrils clos'd up:
To teach mortal worms the path
That leads from the gates of the grave.'

But, in the darkness of their 'ancient woven dens,' they are startled by 'the thick-flaming, thought-creating fires of Orc'; and at their cry Urizen comes forth to meet and challenge the liberating spirit; he thunders against the pillar of fire that rises out of the darkness of Europe; and at the clash of their mutual onset 'the Grave shrieks aloud.' But 'Urizen wept,' the cold pity of reason which, as we have seen in the book named after him, freezes into nets of religion, 'twisted like to the human brain.'

The Book of Los (also dated 1795) is written in the short lines of Urizen and Ahania, a metre following a fixed, insistent beat, as of Los's hammer on his anvil. It begins with the lament of 'Eno, aged Mother,' over the liberty of old times:

> 'O Times remote!
> When Love and Joy were adoration,
> And none impure were deem'd.
> Not Eyeless Covet,
> Nor Thin-lip'd Envy,
> Nor Bristled Wrath,
> Nor Curled Wantonness;'

none of these, that is, yet turned to evil, but still unfallen energies. At this, flames of desire break out, 'living, intelligent,' and Los, the spirit of Inspiration, divides the flames, freezes them into solid darkness, and is imprisoned by them, and escapes, only in terror, and falls through ages into the void ('Truth has bounds, Error none'), until he has organised the void and brought into it a light which makes visible the form of the void. He sees it as the backbone of Urizen, the bony outlines of reason, and then begins,for the first time in the Prophetic Books, that building of furnaces, and wielding of hammer and anvil of which we are to hear so much in *Jerusalem*. He forges the sun and chains cold intellect to vital heat, from whose torments

> 'a twin
> Was completed, a Human Illusion
> In darkness and deep clouds involved.'

In *The Book of Los* there is a minute exquisiteness of design and colour: faint, delicately varied washes, full of dull radiance. In the ghastly crouching figure of the frontispiece, with its crushing feet, there is a strange vast precision of outline, as of a primeval monster faithfully copied; the background and the ground under its feet is of lovely colour, a dull splendour, as if the brightest colours had been subdued by an impending darkness. There is a vaguer suggestion, still colour emotional in its meaning, in the design on the title-page. A piece of pure gaiety, incredibly intricate, is woven out of the lettering of the world Los at the beginning of the poem; and at the end there is an outburst of subdued radiance—a red sun glowing among clouds of sunrise and an exultant angel with arms and legs outspread above in the upper heaven.

The Song of Los is violent and astounding—a new technique—colour laid on roughly—colour crackling and surging; with stabs of red across green, hieroglyphic suns bursting into wheels of blue sun-rays over figures of grotesque giants, fairies and a sort of bloated body or *cul-de-jatte*, with a black hammer outside a blood-red sun barred by black clouds. This is the final page: a nightmare, a horror, bursting with blood.

Bloody serpents twine across the the pages, fires of all colour, wild foliage and leafage, lakes of blue darkness, deserts of sunset–coloured rock and sand, over which wild figures race embraced; and in the midst a full page of the King and Queen of the Fairies resting romantically on the broad leaves of tall plants against a sky of white stars.

Asia begins with a circling stream, like a river of many-coloured fires, flowing under a red dawn or sunset, with helpless, bowed human figures screened in hollow caves under the water, or stooping on enormous kness under safe branches. The trees of flame which twine across the last page are lovely in their poisonous vegetation, full of delicate suggestions of leaf and branch. They have the ardour of a vast overcoming outgrowth bursting across the world. At the end are putrid jewels of profound ecstasy, the Ecstasy of Evil.

In *The Book of Los* almost all relationship to poetry has vanished; the myth is cloudier and more abstract. Scarcely less so is *The Book of Ahania* (1795), written in the same short lines, but in a manner occasionally more concrete and realisable. Like *Urizen*, it is almost all myth. It follows Fuzon, 'son of Urizen's silent burnings,' in his fiery revolt against

> 'This cloudy God seated on waters,
> Now seen, now obscured, king of Sorrows.'

From the stricken and divided Urizen is born Ahania ('so name his parted soul'), who is 'his invisible lust,' whom he loves, hides, and calls Sin.

> 'She fell down, a faint shadow wandering,
> In chaos, and circling dark Urizen,
> As the moon anguished circles the earth,
> Hopeless, abhorred, a death shadow,

Unseen, unbodied, unknown,
The mother of Pestilence.'

But Urizen, recovering his strength, seizes the bright son of fire, his energy or passion, and nails him to the dark 'religious' 'Tree of Mystery,' from under whose shade comes the voice of Ahania, 'weeping upon the void,' lamenting her lost joys of love, and the days when,

'Swelled with ripeness and fat with fatness,
Bursting on winds my odours,
My ripe figs and rich pomegranates,
In infant joy at my feet,
O Urizen, sported and sang.'

In *The Four Zoas* Ahania is called 'the feminine indolent bliss, the indulgent self of weariness.' 'One final glimpse,' says Swinburne, 'we may take of Ahania after her division—the love of God, as it were, parted from God, impotent therefore and a shadow, if not rather a plague and blight; mercy severed from justice, and thus made a worse thing than useless.' And her lament ends in this despair:

'But now alone over rocks, mountains,
Cast out from thy lovely bosom
Cruel jealousy, selfish fear,
Self-destroying; how can delight
Renew in these chains of darkness
Where bones of beasts are strown
On the bleak and snowy mountains,
Where bones from the birth are buried
Before they see the light.'

The mythology, of which parts are developed in each of these books, is thrown together, in something more approaching a whole, but without apparent cohesion or consistency, in *The Four Zoas*, which probably dates from 1797 and which exists in seventy sheets of manuscript, of uncertain order, almost certainly in an unfinished state, perhaps never intended for publication, but rather as a storehouse of ideas. This manuscript, much altered, arranged in a conjectural order, and printed with extreme incorrectness, was published by Messrs. Ellis and Yeats in the third volume of their book on Blake, under the first, rejected, title of *Vala*.[1] They describe it as being in itself a sort of compound of all Blake's other books, except *Milton* and *Jerusalem*, which are enriched by scraps taken from *Vala*, but are not summarised in it. In the uncertain state in which we have it, it is impossible to take it as a wholly authentic text; but it is both full of incidental beauty and of considerable assistance in unravelling many of the mysteries in *Milton* and *Jerusalem*, the books written at Felpham, both dated 1804, in which we find the final development of the myth, or as much of that final development as has come to us in the absence of the manuscripts destroyed or disposed of by Tatham. Those two books indeed seem to presuppose in their readers an acquaintance with many matters told or explained in this, from which passages are taken bodily, but with little apparent method. As it stands, *Vala* is much more of a poem than either *Milton* or *Jerusalem*; the cipher comes in at times, but between there are broad spaces of cloudy but not wholly unlighted imagery. Blake still remembers that he is writing a poem, earthly beauty is still divine beauty to him, and the message is not yet so stringent as to forbid all lingering by the way.

In some parts of the poem the manner is frankly biblical, and suggests the book of Proverbs, as thus:

'What is the price of experience? Do men buy it for a song,
Or wisdom for a dance in the street? No, it is bought with the price
Of all that a man hath—his wife, his house, his children.
Wisdom is sold in the desolate market where none comes to buy,
And in the withered fields where the farmer ploughs for bread in vain.'

Nature is still an image accepted as an adequate symbol, and we get reminiscences here and there of the simpler, early work of *Thel*, for instance, in such lines as:

'And as the little seed waits eagerly watching for its flower and fruit,
Anxious its little soul looks out into the clear expanse
To see if hungry winds are abroad with their invisible array;
So man looks out in tree and herb, and fish and bird and beast,

1. The text of *Vala*, with corrections and additional errors, is now accessible in the second volume of Ellis's edition of Blake's *Poetical Works*.

Collecting up the scattered portions of his immortal body
Into the elemental forms of everything that grows.'

There are descriptions of feasts, of flames, of last judgments, of the new Eden, which are full of colour and splendour, passing without warning into the 'material sublime' of Fuseli, as in the picture of Urizen 'stonied upon his throne' in the eighth 'Night.' In the passages which we possess in the earlier and later version we see the myth of Blake gradually crystallising, the transposition of every intelligible symbol into the secret cipher. Thus we find 'Mount Gilead' changed into 'Mount Snowdon,' 'Beth Peor' into 'Cosway Vale,' and a plain image such as this:

'The Mountain called out to the Mountain, Awake, oh brother Mountain,'

is translated backwards into:

' Ephraim called out to Tiriel, Awake, oh brother Mountain.'

Images everywhere are seen freezing into types; they stop half-way, and have not yet abandoned the obscure poetry of the earlier Prophetic Books for the harder algebra of *Milton* and *Jerusalem*.

CHAPTER VI

To those who really care for Blake almost anything connected with him is of interest, and in the scraps which follow it seems to me that we get several glimpses of him in passing. The first statement by Blake of his aims and principles in art is to be found in some letters to George Cumberland and to Dr. Trusler, contained in the Cumberland Papers in the British Museum. These letters were first printed by Dr. Garnett in the *Hampstead Annual* of 1903, but with many mistakes and omissions.[1]

A large part of the letters in the Cumberland Papers are written by Cumberland to his son George, or by George to his father, and two of these relating to Blake, are given by Dr. Garnett in the *Hampstead Annual*. The whole series is full of entertainment, and is like a novel in chapters written after Richardson with humours, crudities and moralizings worthly of *Pamela*. George Cumberland was a Bristol gentleman who was a good friend to many artists, and he would appear to have written at least on novel about which persons as unlike as Taylor of Norwich and Richard Cromek were equally exercised in mind. Thomas Taylor, in one of several quaint letters, writes on 16 October, 1798:

'With respect to your novel, since you desire me to give you my opinion freely of its merit, I must own that I think it more entertaining than instructive, more ingenious than moral to defend lasciviousness publickly; and yet to me it appears that it is as much patronized by the conduct of your Sophisms, as by the works of Mrs. Woolstoncraft. You will doubtless excuse the freedom of this Opinion, when you consider that as I am a professed Platonist, love is with me true only in proportion as it is *pure*; or, in proportion as it rises above the gratification of our brutal part.'

It is apparently to the same novel that Cromek refers in a letter written in the year of his publication of Blake's 'inventions'

1. They are now to be read in Mr. Russell's edition of *The Letters of William Blake*.

in illustration of Blair's *Grave*. The story of the quarrel between Blake and Cromek has been amply enough explained elsewhere, and most cogently by Swinburne in his book on Blake; but there is enough evidence of character and manners in this mere business letter to account for the whole quarrel. Cromek writes to Cumberland:

'MY DEAR SIR,

'With this you will receive the Book you had ye goodness to subscribe for.

'I should feel myself much wanting in gratitude if I did not beg your acceptance of this book as an acknowledgement, at least, of the many kindnesses I received from you and your good Family when in Bristol.

'Through the d — d carelessness of my Printer your Name is omitted in the list; a misfortune that I deplored, and almost raved about for theree Days and three Nights.

'You are one of ye only persons in Bristol who thoroughly understands the Inventions of Blake — your Name has also some influence, and consequently the affair is to the last degree unlucky. However it is past.

'Of *course* our Friend Stothard has not written to thank you for your Drawings — but, I can assure you, he is very thankful for them, and seemed much pleased with your attention.

'Your other little Parcels have been safely delivered.

'Touching your printed Book, I can do nothing about it. It is generally thought that the descriptions are too *luxuriant*. I shall be at Bristol about Decr, and will bring it with me.

'I need not ask you to speak of the Book as you may think it ought to be spoken of.

'With respectful Compts. to Mrs. Cumberland and your family.

'I remain

'My Dear Sir

'Your obt. hble. Servt.

'R. H. CROMEK.

'64 NEWMAN ST., LONDON, *Aug. 14-th*, 1808

'Your Packet went to Blake. I sent him 2 Copies, but he has not had the common politeness to thank me for them.'

It was at Cromek's house that young Cumberland was for a time boarded, and he complains that the Cromeks, by 'their selfish dispositions,' are 'true Yorkshire.' It is at Cromek's that he receives a letter dated 2 December, 1808, in which his father says: 'I send Blake the Drawings by Giorgiana... I send Mr. Blake a few old Tracings from Raffaels Pictures in Fresco. I shall keep a great many for you—and when you come to Draw a little send them up to you a few at a time—send them to Blake the first opportunity as things of little value to him, being rude sketches only—those I keep for you are the best.'

The son replies, on 4 December: 'Mr. Blake was very much pleased with the Traicings. I thought it a good opportunity to ask him for the Holy Family, which he gave very readily.' The father, writing on the 12th, corrects: 'Tracings not traicings,' and adds: 'I hope you did not ask Blake for the Picture very *importunately*. I must send him more of these heads–a few I keep for you. I shall retrace them all in Ink.'

The curious reference in a letter dated 22 January, 1809, I cannot identify: 'Tell *Blake* a Mr. Sivewright of Edinburgh has just claimed in Home Philosophical Journal of last month as his own invention Blakes Method—and call it Copper Blocks I think,' In the same year there is a letter from the son to the father, dated from the Pay Office, Whitehall, 14 October, 1809, in which he says, in his slovenly way: 'Blakes has published a Catalogue of Pictures beings the ancient method of Frescoe Painting *Restored*. You should tell Mr. Barry to get it, it may be the means of serving your friend. It sells for *2s. 6d.* and may be had of J. Blake, 28 Broad St., Golden Square, at his brothers—the Book is a great curiosity. He as *(sic)* given Stothard a compleet set down.' The father immediately writes: 'Send by Mr. Grindon 2 vols. of Blake's work and make my regard to Blake.' It is not always that young George presents himself to us in a quite amiable light; but here, in this friendly taking of sides, I seem to see in him some of the virtues of the partisan.

It appears that in the year 1799 Blake undertook, at the suggestion of Cumberland, to do some drawings for a book by Dr. Trusler, a sort of quack writer and publisher, who may be perhaps sufficiently defined by the quotation of the title of one of his books, which is *The Way to be Rich and Respectable*. On August 16, Blake writes to say: 'I find more and more that my Style of Designing is a Species by itself, and in this which I send you have been compelled by my Genius or Angel to follow where he led; if I were to act otherwise it would not fulfil the purpose for which alone I live, which is in conjunction with such men as my friend Cumberland to renew the lost Art of the Greeks.' He tells him that he has attempted to 'follow his Dictate' every morning for a fortnight, but 'it was out of my power!' He then describes what he has done, and says: 'If you approve of my manner, and it is agreeable to you, I would rather Paint Pictures in oil of the same dimensions than make Drawings, and on the same terms. By this means you will have a number of Cabinet pictures, which I flatter myself will not be unworthy of a Scholar of Rembrant and Teniers, whom I have Studied no less than Rafael and Michaelangelo.'

The next letter, which I will give in full, for it is a document of great importance, is dated a week later, and the nature of the reply which it answers can be gathered from Blake's comment on the matter to Cumberland, three days later still. 'I have made him,' he says, 'a Drawing in my best manner: he has sent it back with a Letter full of Criticisms, in which he says It accords not with his Intentions, which are, to Reject all Fancy from his Work. How far he expects to please, I cannot tell. But as I cannot paint Dirty rags and old Shoes where I ought to place Naked Beauty or simple ornament, I despair of ever pleasing one Class of Men.' 'I could not help smiling,' he says later, 'at the difference between the doctrines of Dr. Trusler and those of Christ.' Here, then, is the letter in which Blake accounts for himself to the quack doctor (who has docketed it: 'Blake, Dimd with superstition'), as if to posterity:

'REVD. SIR,

'I really am sorry that you are falln out with the Spiritual World, Especially if I should have to answer for it. I feel very sorry that your Ideas and Mine on Moral Painting differ so much as to have made you angry with my method of study. If I am wrong I am wrong in good company. I had hoped your plan comprehended All Species of this Art, and Especially that you would not regret that Species which gives Existence to Every other, namely, Visions of Eternity. You say that I want somebody to Elucidate my Ideas. But you ought to know that what is Grand is necessarily obscure to Weak men. That which can be made Explicit to the Ideot is not worth my care. The wisest of the Ancients considerd what is not too Explicit as the fittest for Instruction, because it rouzes the faculties to act. I name Moses, Solomon, Esop, Homer, Plato.

'But as you have favord me with your remarks on my Design, permit me in return to defend it against a mistaken one, which is, That I have supposed Malevolence without a Cause. Is not Merit in one a Cause of Envy in another, and Serenity and Happiness and Beauty a Cause of Malevolence? But Want of Money and the Distress of a Thief can never be alledged as the Cause of his Thievery, for many honest people endure greater hardships with Fortitude. We must therefore seek the Cause elsewhere than in the want of Money, for that is the Miser's passion, not the Thief's.

'I have therefore proved your Reasonings Ill proportioned, which you can never prove my figures to be. They are those of Michael Angelo, Rafael and the Antique, and of the best living Models. I perceive that your Eye is perverted by Caricature Prints, which ought not to abound so much as they do. Fun I love, but too much Fun is of all things the most loathsome. Mirth is better than Fun, and Happiness is better than Mirth. I feel that a Man may be happy in This World, and I know that This World is a World of Imagination and Vision. I see Everything I paint In This World: but Every body does not see alike. To the Eyes of a Miser a Guinea is more beautiful than the Sun, and a bag worn with the use of Money has more beautiful proportions than a Vine filled with Grapes. The tree which moves some to tears of joy is in the Eyes of others only a Green thing that stands in the way. Some see Nature all Ridicule and Deformity, and by these I shall not regulate my proportions; and some scarce see Nature at all. But to the Eyes of the Man of Imagination, Nature is Imagination itself. As a Man is, so he sees. As the Eye is formed, such are its Powers. You certainly Mistake when you say that the Visions of Fancy are not to be found in This World. To Me This World is all One continued Vision of Fancy or Imagination, and I feel Flattered when I am told so. What is it sets Homer, Virgil, and Milton in so high a rank of Art? Why is the Bible more Entertaining and Instructive than any other book? Is it not because they are addressed to the Imagination, which is Spiritual Sensation, and but mediately to the Understanding or Reason? Such is True Painting, and such was alone valued by the Greeks and the best modern Artists. Consider what Lord Bacon says—'Sense sends over to Imagination before Reason have judged, and Reason sends over to Imagination before the Decree can be acted.' See *Advancement of Learning*, Part 2, P. 47, of first Edition.

But I am happy to find a Great Majority of Fellow Mortals who can Elucidate My Visions, and Particularly they have been Elucidated by Children, who have taken a greater delight in contemplating my Pictures than I even hoped. Neither Youth nor Childhood is Folly or Incapacity. Some Children are Fools, and so are some old Men. But There is a vast Majority on the side of Imagination or Spiritual Sensation.

To Engrave after another Painter is infinitely more laborious than to Engrave one's own Inventions. And of the size you require my price has been Thirty Guineas, and I cannot afford to do it for less. I had Twelve for the Head I sent you as a Specimen; but after my own designs I could do at least Six times the quantity of labour in the same time, which will account for the difference in price, as also that Chalk Engraving is at least Six times as laborious as Aqua tinta. I have no objection to Engraving after another Artist. Engraving is the profession I was apprenticed to, and I should never have attempted to live by any thing else If orders had not come in for my Designs and Paintings, which I have the pleasure to tell you are Increasing Every Day. Thus If I am a Painter it is not to be attributed to Seeking after. But I am contented whether I live by Painting or Engraving.

'I am, Revd. Sir, your very obedient Servant,

'WILLIAM BLAKE.

'13 HERCULES BUILDINGS, LAMBETH,
'*August* 23, 1799.'

There are many stories of Blake's love of children, and of their love for him, but this is the only reference that I have found in his own writings to his belief in a child's faculty of seeing spiritually, and to his consciousness of children's delight in his pictures.

Blake tells Cumberland the whole story quite cheerfully, and ends with these significant words, full of patience, courtesy, and sad humour: 'As to Myself, about whom you are so kindly Interested, I live by Miracle. I am Painting small Pictures from the Bible. For as to Engraving, in which art I cannot reproach myself with any neglect, yet I am laid by in a corner as if I did not exist, and since my Young's *Night Thoughts* have been published, even Johnson and Fuseli have discarded my Graver. But as I know that He who works and has his health cannot starve, I laugh at Fortune and Go on and on. I think I foresee better Things than I have ever seen. My Work pleases my employer, and I have an order for Fifty small Pictures at One Guinea each, which is something better than mere copying after another artist. But above all I feel myself happy and contented, let what will come. Having passed now near twenty years in ups and downs, I am used to them, and perhaps a little practice in them may turn out to benefit. It is now exactly Twenty years since I was upon the ocean of business, and tho I laugh at Fortune, I am persuaded that She Alone is the Governor of Worldly Riches, and when it is Fit She will call on me. Till then I wait with Patience, in hopes that She is busied among my Friends.'

The employer is, no doubt, Mr. Butts, for whom Blake had already begun to work: we know some of the 'frescoes' and colour-prints which belong to this time; among them, or only just after, the incomparable 'Crucifixion,' in which the soldiers cast lots in the foreground and the crosses are seen from the back, against a stormy sky and lances like Tintoretto's. But it was also the time of all but the latest Prophetic Books (or of all but the latest of those left to us), and we may pause here for a moment to consider some of the qualities that Blake was by this time fully displaying in his linear and coloured inventions and 'Visions of Eternity.'

It is by his energy and nobility of creation that Blake takes rank among great artists, in a place apart from those who have been content to study, to observe, and to copy. His invention of living form is like Nature's, unintermittent, but without the measure and order of Nature, and without complete command over the material out of which it creates. In his youth he had sought after prints of such inventive work as especially appealed to him, Michelangelo, Raphael, Dürer; it is possible that, having had 'very early in life the ordinary opportunities,' as Dr. Malkin puts it, 'of seeing pictures in the houses of noblemen and gentlemen, and in the king's palaces,' he had seen either pictures, or prints after pictures, of the Italian Primitives, whose attitudes and composition he at times suggests; and, to the end, he worked with Dürer's 'Melancholia' on his work-table and Michelangelo's designs on his walls. It not unfrequently happened that a memory of form created by one of these great draughtsmen presented itself as a sort of short cut to the statement of the form which he was seeing or creating in his own imagination. A Devil's Advocate has pointed out 'plagiarisms' in Blake's design, and would dismiss in consequence his reputation for originality. Blake had not sufficient mastery of technique to be always wholly original in design; and it is to his dependence on a technique not as flexible as his imagination was intense that we must attribute what is unsatisfying in such remarkable inventions as 'The House of Death' (Milton's lazar-house) in the Print Room of the British Museum. Its appeal to the imagination is partly in spite of what is 'organised and minutely articulated beyond all that the mortal and perishing nature can produce.' Death is a version of the Ancient of Days and of Urizen, only his eyes are turned to blind terror and his beard to forked flame; Despair, a statue of greenish bronze, is the Scofield of *Jerusalem*; the limbs and faces rigid with agony are types of strength and symbols of pain. Yet even here there is creation, there is the energy of life, there is a spiritual awe. And wherever Blake works freely, as in the regions of the Prophetic Books, wholly outside time and space, appropriate form multiplies under his creating hand, as it weaves a new creation of worlds and of spirits, monstrous and angelical.

Blake distinguished, as all great imaginative artists have distinguished, between allegory, which is but realism's excuse for existence, and symbol, which is none of the 'daughters of Memory,' but itself vision or inspiration. He wrote in the MS. book: 'Vision or imagination is a representation of what actually exists, really and unchangeably. Fable or allegory is formed by the daughters of Memory.' And thus in the designs which accompany the text of his Prophetic Books there is rarely the mere illustration of those pages. He does not copy in line what he has said in words, or explain in words what he has rendered in line; a creation probably contemporary is going on, and words and lines render between them, the one to the eyes, the other to the mind, the same image of spiritual things, apprehended by different organs of perception.

And so in his pictures, what he gives us is not a picture after a mental idea; it is the literal delineation of an imaginative vision, of a conception of the imagination. He wrote: 'If you have not nature before you for every touch, you cannot paint portrait; and if you have nature before you at all, you cannot paint history.' There is a water-colour of Christ in the carpenter's shop: Christ, a child, sets to the floor that compass which Blake saw more often in the hands of God the Father, stooping out of heaven; his mother and Joseph stand on each side of him, leaning towards him with the stiff elegance of guardian angels on a tomb. That is how Blake sees it, and not with the minute detail and the aim at local colour with which the Pre-Raphaelites have seen it; it is not Holman Hunt's 'Bethlehem' nor the little Italian town of Giotto; it is rendered carefully after the visual imagination which the verses of the Bible awakened in his brain. In one of those variations which he did on the 'Flight into Egypt' (the 'Riposo,' as he called it), we have a lovely and surprising invention of landscape, minute and impossible, with a tree built up like a huge vegetable, and flowers growing out of the bare rock, and a red and flattened sun going down behind the hills; Joseph stands under the tree, nearly of the same height, but grave and kindly, and the Mother and Child are mild eighteenth-century types of innocence; the browsing donkey has an engaging rough homeliness of hide and aspect. It is all as unreal as you like, made up of elements not combined into any faultless pattern; art has gone back further than Giotto, and is careless of human individuality; but it is seen as it were with faith, and it conveys to you precisely what the painter meant to convey. So, in a lovely water-colour of the creation of Eve, this blue-haired doll of obviously rounded flesh has in her something which is more as well as less than the appeal of bodily beauty, some suggestion to the imagination which the actual technical skill of Blake has put there. With less delicacy of colour, and with drawing in parts actually misleading, there is a strange intensity of appeal, of realisation not so much to the eyes as through them to the imagination, in another water-colour of the raising of Lazarus, where the corpse swathed in grave-clothes, floats sidelong upward from the grave, the weight of mortality as if taken off, and an unearthly lightness in its disemprisoned limbs, that have forgotten the laws of mortal gravity.

Yet, even in these renderings of what is certainly not meant for reality, how abundantly nature comes into the design: mere bright parrot-like birds in the branches of the tree of knowledge of good and evil, the donkey of the 'Riposo,' the sheep's heads woven into the almost decorative border. Blake was constantly on his guard against the deceits of nature, the temptation of a 'facsimile representation of merely mortal and perishing substances.' His dread of nature was partly the recoil of his love; he feared to be entangled in the 'veils of Vala,' the seductive sights of the world of the senses; and his love of natural things is evident on every page of even the latest of the Prophetic Books. It is the natural world, the idols of Satan, that creep in at every corner and border, setting flowers to grow, and birds to fly, and snakes to glide harmlessly around the edges of these hard and impenetrable pages. The minute life of this 'vegetable world' is awake and in subtle motion in the midst of these cold abstractions. 'The Vegetable World opens like a flower from the Earth's centre, in which is Eternity,' and it is this outward flowering of eternity in the delicate living forms of time that goes on incessantly, as if by the mere accident of the creative impulse, as Blake or Los builds Golgonooza or the City of God out of the 'abstract void' and the 'indefiniteness of unimaginative existence.' It is, on every page, the visible outer part of what, in the words, can but speak a language not even meant to be the language of the 'natural man.'

In these symbolic notations of nature, or double language of words and signs, these little figures of men and beasts that so strangely and incalculably decorate so many of Blake's pages, there is something Egyptian, which reminds me of those lovely riddles on papyri and funeral tablets, where the images of real things are used so decoratively, in the midst of a language itself all pictures, with colours never seen in the things themselves, but given to them for ornament. *The Marriage of Heaven and Hell* is filled with what seem like the hieroglyphics on an Egyptian tomb or obelisk, little images which might well mean things as definite as the images of Egyptian writing. They are still visible, sometimes mere curves or twines, in the latest of the engraved work, and might exist equally for some symbolic life which they contain, or for that decorative life of design which makes them as expressive mosaics of pattern as the hieroglyphics. I cannot but think that it was partly from what he had seen, in actual basalt, or in engravings after ancient monuments which must have been about him at Basire's the engraver's, that Blake found the suggestion of his picture-writing in the Prophetic Books. He believed that all Greek art was but a pale copy of a lost art of Egypt, 'the greater works of the Asiatic Patriarchs,' 'Apotheoses of Persian, Hindu, and Egyptian antiquity.' In such pictures as 'The Spiritual Form of Pitt guiding Behemoth,' he professed to be but 'applying to modern heroes, on a smaller scale,' what he had seen in vision of these 'stupendous originals now lost, or perhaps buried till some happier age.' Is it not likely therefore that in his attempt to create the religious books of a new religion, 'the Everlasting Gospel' of the Poetic Genius, which is the Lord,' he should have turned to the then unintelligible forms in which the oldest of the religions had written itself down in a visible pictorial message?

But, whatever suggestions may have come to him from elsewhere, Blake's genius was essentially Gothic, and took form, I doubt not, during those six years of youth when he drew the monuments in Westminster Abbey, and in the old churches about London. He might have learned much from the tombs in the Abbey, and from the brasses, and from the carved angels in the chapels, and from the naïve groups on the screen in the chapel of Edward the Confessor, and from the draped figures round the sarcophagus of Amyer de Valence. There is often, in Blake's figures, something of the monumental stiffness of Gothic stone, as there is in the minute yet formal characterisation of the faces. His rendering of terrible and evil things, the animal beings who typify the passions and fierce distortions of the soul, have the same childlike detail, content to be ludicrous if it can only be faithful to a distinct conception, of the carvers of gargoyles and of Last Judgments. Blake has, too, the same love of pattern for its own sake, the same exuberance of ornament, always living and organic, growing out of the structure of the design or out of the form of the page, not added to it from without. Gothic art taught him his hatred of vacant space, his love of twining and trailing foliage and flame and water; and his invention of ornament is as unlimited as theirs. A page of one of his illuminated books is like the carving on a Gothic capital. Lines uncoil from a hidden centre and spread like branches or burst into vast vegetation, emanating from leaf to limb, and growing upward into images of human and celestial existence. The snake is in all his designs; whether, in *Jerusalem,* rolled into chariot-wheels and into the harness of a chariot drawn by hoofed lions, and into the curled horns of the lions, and into the pointing fingers of the horns; or, in *The Marriage of Heaven and Hell,* a leviathan of the sea with open jaws, eyed and scaled with poisonous jewels of purple and blood-red and corroded gold, swelling visibly out of a dark sea that foams aside from its passage; or, curved above the limbs and wound about the head of a falling figure in lovely diminishing coils like a corkscrew which is a note of interrogation; or, in mere unterrifying beauty, trailed like a branch of a bending tree across the tops of pages; or, bitted and bridled and a thing of blithe gaiety, ridden by little, naked, long-legged girls and boys in the new paradise of an America of the future. The Gothic carvers loved snakes, but hardly with the strange passion of Blake. They carved the flames of hell and of earthly punishment with delight in the beauty of their soaring and twisting lines; but no one has ever made of fire such a plaything and ecstasy as Blake has made of it. In his paintings he invents new colours to show forth the very soul of fire, a soul angrier and more variable than opals; and in his drawings he shows us lines and nooses of fire rushing upward out of the ground, and fire drifting across the air like vapour, and fire consuming the world in the last chaos. And everywhere there are gentle and caressing tongues and trails of fire, hardly to be distinguished from branches of trees and blades of grass and stems and petals of flowers. Water, which the Gothic carvers represented in curving lines, as the Japanese do, is in Blake a not less frequent method of decoration; wrapping frail human figures in wet caverns under the depths of the sea, and destroying and creating worlds.

Blake's colour is unearthly, and is used for the most part rather as a symbol of emotion than as a representation of fact. It is at one time prismatic, and radiates in broad bands of pure colour; at another, and more often, is as inextricable as the veins in mineral, and seems more like a natural growth of the earth than the creation of a painter. In the smaller Book of Designs in the Print Room of the British Museum the colours have mouldered away, and blotted themselves together in a sort of putrefaction which seems to carry the suggestions of poisonous decay further than Blake carried them. This will be seen by a comparison of the minutely drawn leviathan of *The Marriage of Heaven and Hell*, with the coloured print in the Book of Designs, in which the outline of the folds melts and crumbles into a mere chaos of horror. Colour in Blake is never shaded, or, as he would have said, blotted and blurred; it is always pure energy. In the faint colouring of *The Book of Thel* there is the very essence of gentleness; the colour is a faultless interpretation of the faint and lovely monotony of the verse, and of its exquisite detail. Several of the plates recur in the Book of Designs, coloured at a different and, no doubt, much later time; and while every line is the same the whole atmosphere and mood of the designs is changed. Bright rich colour is built up in all the vacant spaces; and with the colour there comes a new intensity; each design is seen over again, in a new way. Here, the mood is a wholly different mood, and this seeing by contraries is easier to understand than when, as in the splendid design on the fourth page of *The Book of Urizen*, repeated in the Book of Designs, we see a parallel, yet different, vision, a new, yet not contrary, aspect. In the one, the colours of the open book are like corroded iron or rusty minerals; in the other, sharp blues, like the wings of strange butterflies, glitter stormily under the red flashes of a sunset. The vision is the same, but every colour of the thing seen is different.

To Blake, colour is the soul rather than the body of his figures, and seems to clothe them like an emanation. What Behmen says of the world itself might be said of Blake's rendering of the aspects of the world and men. 'The whole outward visible World,' he tells us, 'with all its Being is a Signature, or Figure of the inward spiritual World; whatever is internally, and however its Operation is, so likewise it has its Character externally; like as the Spirit of each Creature sets forth and manifests the internal Form of its Birth, by its Body, so does the Eternal Being also.' Just as he gives us a naked Apollo for the 'spiritual form of Pitt' in the picture in the National Gallery, where Pitt is seen guiding Behemoth, or the hosts of evil, in a hell of glowing and obscure tumult, so he sees the soul of a thing or being with no relation to its normal earthly colour. The colours of fire and of blood, an extra-lunar gold, putrescent vegetable colours, and the stains in rocks and sunsets, he sees everywhere, and renders with an ecstasy that no painter to whom colour was valuable for its own sake has ever attained. It is difficult not to believe that he does not often use colour with a definitely musical sense of its harmonies, and that colour did not literally sing to him, as it seems, at least in a permissible figure, to sing to us out of his pages.

CHAPTER VII

At the end of September 1800 Blake left Lambeth, and took a cottage at Felpham, near Bognor, at the suggestion of William Hayley, the feeblest poet of his period, who imagined, with foolish kindness, that he could become the patron of one whom he called 'my gentle visionary Blake.' Hayley was a rich man, and, as the author of *The Triumphs of Temper*, was looked upon as a person of literary importance. He did his best to give Blake opportunities of making money, by doing engraving and by painting miniatures of the neighbours. He read Greek with him and Klopstock. 'Blake is just become a Grecian, and literally learning the language,' he says in one letter, and in another: 'Read Klopstock into English to Blake.' The effect of Klopstock on Blake is to be seen in a poem of ribald magnificence, which no one has yet ventured to print in full. The effect of Blake on Hayley, and of Hayley on Blake, can be realised from a few passages in the letters. At first we read: 'Mr. Hayley acts like a prince.' Then: 'I find on all hands great objections to my doing anything but the mere drudgery of business, and intimations that, if I do not confine myself to this, I shall not live.' Last: 'Mr. H. is as much averse to my poetry as he is to a chapter in the Bible. He knows that I have writ it, for I have shown it to him' (this is apparently the *Milton* or the *Jerusalem*), 'and he has read part by his own desire, and has looked with sufficient contempt to enhance my opinion of it. ... But Mr. H. approves of my designs as little as he does of my poems, and I have been forced to insist on his leaving me, in both, to my own self-will; for I am determined to be no longer pestered with his genteel ignorance and polite disapprobation. I know myself both poet and painter, and it is not his affected contempt that can move to anything but a more assiduous pursuit of both arts. Indeed, by my late firmness I have brought down his affected loftiness, and he begins to think that I have some genius: as if genius and assurance were the same thing! But his imbecile attempts to depress me only deserve laughter.' What laughter they produced, while Blake was still suffering under them, can be seen by any one who turns to the epigrams on H. in the note-book. But the letter goes on, with indignant seriousness: 'But I was commanded by my spiritual friends to bear all and be silent, and to go through all without murmuring, and, in fine, hope till my three years shall be accomplished; at which time I was set at liberty to remonstrate against former conduct, and to demand justice and truth; which I have done in so effectual a manner that my antagonist is silenced completely, and I have compelled what should have been of freedom—my just right as an artist and as a man.'

In Blake's behaviour towards Hayley, which has been criticised, we can test his sincerity to himself under all circumstances: his impeccable outward courtesy, his concessions, 'bearing insulting benevolence' meekly, his careful kindness towards Hayley and hard labour on his behalf, until the conviction was forced upon him from within that 'corporeal friends were spiritual enemies,' and that Hayley must be given up.

'Remembering the verses that Hayley sung
When my heart knocked against the roof of my tongue,'

Blake wrote down bitter epigrams, which were written down for mere relief of mind, and certainly never intended for publication; and I can see no contradiction between these inner revolts and an outer politeness which had in it its due measure of gratitude. Both were strictly true, and only in a weak and foolish nature can the consciousness of kindness received distract or blot out the consciousness of the intellectual imbecility which may lurk behind it. Blake said:

'I never made friends but by spiritual gifts,
By severe contentions of friendship and the burning fire of thought.'

What least 'contention of friendship' would not have been too much for the 'triumphs of temper' of 'Felpham's eldest son'? what 'fire of thought' could ever have enlightened his comfortable darkness? And is it surprising that Blake should have written in final desperation:

'Thy friendship oft has made my heart to ache:
Do be my enemy—for friendship's sake'?

He quarrelled with many of his friends, with those whom he had cared for most, like Stothard and Flaxman; but the cause was always some moral indignation, which, just or unjust, was believed, and which, being believed, could not have been acted upon. With Blake belief and action were simultaneous. 'Thought is Act,' as he wrote on the margin of Bacon's essays.

I am inclined to attribute to this period the writing down of a mysterious manuscript in the possession of Mr. Buxton Forman, which has never been printed, but which, by his kind permission, I have been allowed to read. This manuscript is headed in large lettering: 'The Seven Days of the Created World,' above which is written, as if by an afterthought, in smaller lettering: 'Genesis.' It is written at the beginning of a bluecovered copy-book, of which the paper is water-marked 1797. It consists of some two hundred lines of blank verse, numbered by tens in the margin up to one hundred and fifty, then follow over fifty more lines without numberings, ending without a full stop or any apparent reason for coming to an end. The handwriting is unmistakably Blake's; on the first page or two it is large and careful; gradually it gets smaller and seems more hurried or fatigued, as if it had all been written at a single sitting. The earlier part goes on without a break, but in the later part there are corrections; single words are altered, sometimes as much as a line and a half is crossed out and rewritten, the lines are sometimes corrected in the course of writing. If it were not for these signs of correction I should find it difficult to believe that Blake had actually composed anything so tamely regular in metre or so destitute of imagination or symbol. It is an argument or statement, written in the formal eighteenth-century manner, with pious invocations, God being addressed as 'Sire,' and 'Wisdom Supreme' as his daughter, epithets are inverted that they may fit the better into a line, and geographical names heaped up in a scarcely Miltonic manner, while Ixion strangely neighbours the 'press'd African.' Nowhere is there any characteristic felicity, or any recognizable sign of Blake.

When I saw first the manuscript it occurred to me that it might have been a fragment of translation from Klop-stock, done at Felpham under the immediate dictation of Hayley. 'Read Klopstock into English to Blake' we have seen Hayley noting down. But I can find no original for it in Klopstock. That Blake could have written it out of his own head at any date after 1797 is incredible, even as an experiment in that 'monotonous cadence like that used by Milton and Shakespeare and all writers of English blank verse, derived from the modern bondage of rhyming,' which he tells us in the preface to *Jerusalem* he considered 'to be a necessary and indispensable part of verse,' at the time 'when this verse was first dictated to me.' The only resemblance which we find to it in Blake's published work is in an occasional early fragment like that known as *The Passions*, and where it is so different from this or any of the early attempts at blank verse is in the absolute regularity of the metre. All I can suggest is that Blake may have written it at a very early age, and preserved a rough draft, which Hayley may have induced him to make a clean copy of, and that in the process of copying he may have touched up the metre without altering the main substance. If this is so, I think he stopped so abruptly because he would not, even to oblige Hayley, go on any longer with so uncongenial a task.

Blake's three years at Felpham (September 1800 to September 1803) were described by him as 'my three years' slumber on the banks of ocean,' and there is no doubt that, in spite of the neighbourhood and kindly antagonism of Hayley, that 'slumber' was, for Blake, in a sense an awakening. It was the only period of his life lived out of London, and with Felpham, as he said in a letter to Flaxman, 'begins a new life, because another covering of earth is shaken off.' The cottage at Felpham is only a little way in from a seashore which is one of the loveliest and most changing shores of the English coast. Whistler has painted it, and it is always as full of faint and wandering colour as a Whistler. It was on this coast that Rossetti first learned to care for the sea. To Blake it must have been the realisation of much that he had already divined in his imagination. There, as he wrote to Flaxman, 'heaven opens on all sides her golden gates; her windows are not obstructed by vapours; voices of celestial inhabitants are more distinctly heard and their forms more distinctly seen; and my cottage is also a shadow of their houses.' He drew the cottage on one of the pages of *Milton*, with a naked image of himself walking in the garden, and the image of an angel about to alight on a tree. The cottage is still, as he found it, 'a perfect model for cottages, and I think for palaces of magnificence, only enlarging, not altering its proportions, and adding ornaments and not principles'; and no man of imagination could live there, under that thatched roof and with that marvellous sea before him, and not find himself spiritually naked and within arm's reach of the angels.

The sea has the properties of sleep and of awakening, and there can be no doubt that the sea had both those influences on

Blake, surrounding him for once with an atmosphere like that of his own dreams. 'O lovely Felpham,' he writes, after he had left it, 'to thee I am eternally indebted for my three years' rest from perturbation and the strength I now enjoy.' Felpham represents a vivid pause, in which he had leisure to return upon himself; and in one of his letters he says: 'One thing of real consequence I have accomplished by coming into the country, which is to me consolation enough, namely, I have recollected all my scattered thoughts on art, and resumed my primitive and original ways of execution in both painting and engraving, which in the confusion of London I had very much obliterated from my mind,' It is to this period, no doubt (a period mentally overcome in the quiet of Felpham, but awaiting, as we shall see, the electric spark of that visit to the Truchsessian Gallery in London), that Blake refers in the *Descriptive Catalogue*, when he speaks of the 'experiment pictures' which 'were the result of temptations and perturbations, labouring to destroy imaginative power, by means of that infernal machine, called Chiaro Oscuro, in the hands of Venetian and Flemish demons,' such as the 'outrageous demon,' Rubens, the 'soft and effeminate and cruel demon,' Correggio, and, above all, Titian. 'The spirit of Titian,' we are told, in what is really a confession of Blake's consciousness of the power of those painters whose influence he dreaded, 'was particularly active in raising doubts concerning the possibility of executing without a model; and, when once he had raised the doubt, it became easy for him to snatch away the vision time after tune; for when the artist took his pencil, to execute his ideas, his power of imagination weakened so much, and darkened, that memory of nature and of pictures of the various schools possessed his mind, instead of appropriate execution, resulting from the inventions.' It was thus at Felpham that he returned to himself in art, and it was at Felpham also that he had what seems to have been the culminating outburst of 'prophetic' inspiration, writing from immediate dictation, he said, 'and even against my will.' Visions came readily to him out of the sea, and he saw them walk on the shore, 'majestic shadows, grey but luminous, and superior to the common height of men.'

It was at Felpham that Blake wrote the two last of the Prophetic Books which remain to us, *Milton* and *Jerusalem*. Both bear the date of 1804 on the title-page, and this, no doubt, indicates that the engraving was begun in that year. Yet it is not certain that the engraved text of *Jerusalem*, at any rate, was formally published till after 1809. Pages were certainly inserted between those two dates. On page 38 Blake says:

'I heard in Lambeth's shades:
In Felpham I heard and saw the Visions of Albion:
I write in South Molton Street, what I both see and hear,
In regions of Humanity, in London's opening streets.'

That the main part was writen in Felpham is evident from more than one letter to Butts. In a letter dated April 25, 1803, Blake says: 'But none can know the spiritual acts of my three years' slumber on the banks of ocean, unless he has seen them in the spirit, or unless he should read my long poem descriptive of those acts; for I have in these years composed an immense number of verses on one grand theme, similar to Homer's *Iliad* or Milton's *Paradise Lost*; the persons and machinery entirely new to the inhabitants of earth (some of the persons excepted). I have written the poems from immediate dictation, twelve or sometimes twenty or thirty lines at a time, without premeditation, and even against my will. The time it has taken in writing was thus rendered non-existent, and an immense poem exists which seems to be the labour of a long life, all produced without labour or study. I mention this to show you what I think the grand reason of my being brought down here.' The poem is evidently *Jerusalem*, for the address 'To the Public' on the first page begins: 'After my three years' slumber on the banks of the Ocean, I again Display my Giant forms to the Public.' In the next letter, dated July 6, Blake again refers to the poem: 'Thus I hope that all our three years' trouble ends in good-luck at last, and shall be forgot by my affections, and only remembered by my understanding, to be a memento in time to come, and to speak to future generations by a sublime allegory, which is now perfectly completed into a grand poem. I may praise it, since I dare not pretend to be any other than the secretary; the authors are in eternity. I consider it as the grandest poem that this world contains. Allegory addressed to the intellectual powers, while it is altogether hidden from the corporeal understanding, is my definition of the most sublime poetry. It is somewhat in the same manner defined by Plato. This poem shall, by divine assistance, be progressively printed and ornamented with prints, and given to the public.'

This I take to mean that before Blake's return to London in 1803 the letterpress of *Jerusalem* was, as he imagined, completely finished, but that the printing and illustration were not yet begun. The fact of this delay, and the fact that pages written after 1803 were inserted here and there, must not lead us to think, as many writers on Blake have thought, that there could be any allusion in *Jerusalem* to the attacks of the *Examiner* of 1808 and 1809, or that 'Hand,' one of the wicked sons of Albion, could possibly be, as Rossetti desperately conjectured, 'a hieroglyph for Leigh Hunt.' The sons of Albion are referred to on quite a third of the pages of *Jerusalem*, from the earliest to the latest, and must have been part of the whole texture of the poem from the beginning. In a passage of the 'Public Address,' contained in the Rossetti MS., Blake says: 'The manner in which my character has been blasted these thirty years, both as an artist and as a man, may be seen particularly in a Sunday paper called the *Examiner*, published in Beaufort's Buildings; the manner in which I have rooted out the nest of villains will be seen in a poem concerning my three years' Herculean labours at Felpham, which I shall soon publish.' Even if this is meant for *Jerusalem*, as it may well be, Blake is far from saying that he has referred in the poem to these particular attacks: 'the nest of villains' has undoubtedly a much broader meaning, and groups together all the attacks of thirty years, public or private, of which the *Examiner* is but quoted as a recent example.

The chief reason for supposing that *Jerusalem* may not have been published till after the exhibition of 1809, is to be found in a passage in the *Descriptive Catalogue* which seems to summarise the main subject of the poem, though it is quite possible that it may refer to some MS. now lost. The picture of the Ancient Britons, says Blake, represents three men who 'were originally one man who was fourfold. He was self-divided, and his real humanity slain on the stems of generation, and the form of the fourth was like the Son of God. How he became divided is a subject of great sublimity and pathos. The Artist has written it, under inspiration, and will, if God please, publish it. It is voluminous, and contains the ancient history of Britain, and the world of Satan and Adam.' 'All these things,' he has just said, 'are written in Eden.' And he says further: 'The British Antiquities are now in the Artist's hands; all his visionary contemplations relating to his own country and its ancient glory, when it was, as it again shall be, the source of learning and inspiration.' 'Adam was a Druid, and Noah.' In the description of his picture of the 'Last Judgment' Blake indicates 'Albion, our ancestor, patriarch of the Atlantic Continent, whose history preceded that of the Hebrews, and in whose sleep, or chaos, creation began. The good woman is Britannia, the wife of Albion. Jerusalem is their daughter.'

We see here the symbols, partly Jewish and partly British, into which Blake had gradually resolved his mythology. 'The persons and machinery,' he said, were 'entirely new to the inhabitants of earth (some of the persons excepted).' This has been usually, but needlessly, supposed to mean that real people are introduced under disguises. Does it not rather mean, what would be strictly true, that the 'machinery' is here of a kind wholly new to the Prophetic Books, while of the 'persons' some have already been met with, others are now seen for the first time? It is all, in his own words, 'allegory addressed to the intellectual powers, while it is altogether hidden from the corporeal understanding,' and the allegory becomes harder to read as it becomes more and more naked, concentrated, and unexplained. *Milton* seems to have arisen out of a symbol which came visibly before Blake's eyes on his first waking in the cottage at Felpham. 'Work will go on here with Godspeed,' he writes to Butts. 'A roller and two harrows lie before my window. I met a plough on my first going out at my gate the first morning after my arrival, and the ploughboy said to the ploughman, "Father, the gate is open."' At the beginning of his poem Blake writes:

'The Plow goes forth in tempests and lightnings and the Harrow
 cruel
In blights of the east; the heavy Roller follows in howlings';

and the imagery returns at intervals, in the vision of 'the Last Vintage,' the 'Great Harvest and Vintage of the Nations.' The personal element comes in the continual references to the cottage at Felpham;

'He set me down in Felpham's Vale and prepared a beautiful
Cottage for me that in three years I might write all these Visions
To display Nature's cruel holiness: the deceits of Natural Religion';

and it is in the cottage near the sea that he sees the vision of Milton, when he

'Descended down a Paved work of all kinds of precious stones
Out from the eastern sky; descending down into my Cottage
Garden; clothed in black, severe and silent he descended.'

He awakes from the vision to find his wife by his side:

'My bones trembled. I fell outstretched upon the path
A moment, and my Soul returned into its mortal state
To Resurrection and Judgment in the Vegetable Body,
And my sweet Shadow of delight stood trembling by my side.'

In the prayer to be saved from his friends ('Corporeal Friends are Spiritual Enemies'), in the defence of wrath ('Go to thy labours at the Mills and leave me to my wrath'), in the outburst:

'The idiot Reasoner laughs at the Man of Imagination
And from laughter proceeds to murder by undervaluing calumny,'

it is difficult not to see some trace or transposition of the kind, evil counsellor Hayley, a 'Satan' of mild falsehood in the sight of Blake. But the main aim of the book is the assertion of the supremacy of the imagination:

'The Imagination is not a State: it is the Human Existence itself,'

and the putting off of the 'filthy garments,' of 'Rational Demonstration,' of 'Memory,' of 'Bacon, Locke, and Newton,' the clothing of oneself in imagination,

'To cast aside from Poetry, all that is not Inspiration,
That it shall no longer dare to mock with the aspersion of Madness
Cast on the Inspired by the tame high finisher of paltry Blots,
Indefinite or paltry Ehymes; or paltry harmonies.'

It is because 'Everything in Eternity shines by its own Internal light,' and that jealousy and cruelty and hypocrisy are all darkenings of that light, that Blake declares his purpose of

'Opening to every eye
These wonders of Satan's holiness showing to the Earth
The Idol Virtues of the Natural Heart, and Satan's Seat
Explore in all its Selfish Natural Virtue, and put off
In Self-annihilation all that is not of God alone.'

Such meanings as these flare out from time to time with individual splendours of phrase, like 'Time is the mercy of Eternity,' and the great poetic epigram, 'O Sweden-borg! strongest of men, the Samson shorn by the Churches' (where, for a moment, a line falls into the regular rhythm of poetry), and around them are deserts and jungles, fragments of myth broken off and flung before us after this fashion:

'But Rahab and Tirzah pervert

Their mild influences, therefore the Seven Eyes of God walk round
The Three Heavens of Ulro, where Tirzah and her Sisters
Weave the black Woof of Death upon Entuthon Benython
In the Vale of Surrey where Horeb terminates in Rephaim.'

In '*Jerusalem,* which was to have been 'the grandest poem which the world contains,' there is less of the exquisite lyrical work which still decorates many corners of *Milton,* but it is Blake's most serious attempt to set his myth in order, and it contains much of his deepest wisdom, with astonishing flashes of beauty. In *Milton* there was still a certain approximation to verse, most of the lines had at least a beginning and an end, but in *Jerusalem,* although he tells us that 'every word and every letter is studied and put into its place,' I am by no means sure that Blake ever intended the lines, as he wrote them, to be taken as metrical lines, or read very differently from the prose of the English Bible, with its pause in the sense at the end of each verse. A vague line, hesitating between six and seven beats, does indeed seem from time to time to emerge from chaos, and inversions are brought in at times to accentuate a cadence certainly intended, as here:

'Why should Punishment Weave the Veil with Iron Wheels of War,
When Forgiveness might it Weave with Wings of Cherubim?'

But read the whole book as if it were prose, following the sense for its own sake, and you will find that the prose, when it is not a mere catalogue, has generally a fine biblical roll and swing in it, a rhythm of fine oratory; while if you read each line as if it were meant to be a metrical unit you will come upon such difficulties as this:

'Such is the Forgiveness of the Gods, the Moral Virtues of the '

That is one line, and the next adds 'Heathen.' There may seem to be small reason for such an arrangement of the lines if we read *Jerusalem* in the useful printed text of Mr. Russell and Mr. Maclagan; but the reason will be seen if we turn to the original engraved page, where we shall see that Blake had set down in the margin a lovely little bird with outstretched wings, and that the tip of the bird's wing almost touches the last letter of the 'the' and leaves no room for another word. That such a line was meant to be metrical is unthinkable, as unthinkable as that

'Los stood and stamped the earth, then he threw down his
hammer in rage &
In fury'

has any reason for existing in this form beyond the mere chance of a hand that writes until all the space of a given line is filled. Working as he did within those limits of his hand's space, he would accustom himself to write for the most part, and especially when his imagination was most vitally awake, in lines that came roughly within those limits. Thus it will often happen that the most beautiful passages will have the nearest resemblance to a regular metrical scheme, as in such lines as these:

In vain: he is hurried afar into an unknown Night.
He bleeds in torrents of blood, as he rolls thro' heaven above,
He chokes up the paths of the sky: the Moon is leprous as snow:
Trembling and descending down, seeking to rest on high Mona:
Scattering her leprous snow in flakes of disease over Albion.
The Stars flee remote: the heaven is iron, the earth is sulphur,
And all the mountains and hills shrink up like a withering gourd.'

Here the prophet is no longer speaking with the voice of the orator, but with the old, almost forgotten voice of the poet, and with something of the despised 'Monotonous Cadence.'

In the Prophetic Books Blake labours at the creation of a myth, which may be figured as the representation in space of a vast spiritual tragedy. It is the tragedy of Man, a tragedy in which the first act is creation. Milton was content to begin with 'Man's first disobedience,' but Blake would track the human soul back into chaos, and beyond. He knows, like Krishna, in the *Bhagavad Gita*, that 'above this visible nature there exists another, unseen and eternal, which, when all created things perish, does not perish'; and he sees the soul's birth in that 'inward spiritual world,' from which it falls to mortal life and the body, as into a death. He sees its new, temporal life, hung round with fears and ambushes, out of which, by a new death, the death of that mortal self which separates it from eternity, it may reawaken, even in this life, into the eternal life of imagination. The persons of the drama are the powers and passions of Man, and the spiritual forces which surround him, and are the 'states' through which he passes. Man is seen, as Blake saw all things, fourfold: Man's Humanity; his Spectre, who is Reason, his Emanation, who is

Imagination; his Shadow, who is Desire. And the states through which Man passes, friendly or hostile, energies of good or of evil, are also four: the Four Zoas, who are the Four Living Creatures of Ezekiel, and are called Urizen, Luvah, Tharmas, and Urthona (or, to mortals, Los). Each Zoa has his Emanation: Ahania, who is the emanation of Intellect, and is named 'eternal delight'; Vala, the emanation of Emotion, who is lovely deceit, and the visible beauty of Nature; Enion, who is the emanation of the Senses, and typifies the maternal instinct; Enitharmon, who is the emanation of Intuition, and personifies spiritual beauty. The drama is the division, death, and resurrection, in an eternal circle, of the powers of man and of the powers in whose midst he fights and struggles. Of this incommensurable action we are told only in broken hints, as of a chorus crying outside doors where deeds are being done in darkness. Images pass before us, make their gesture, and are gone; the words spoken are ambiguous, and seem to have an under meaning which it is essential for us to apprehend. We see motions of building and of destruction, higher than the topmost towers of the world, and deeper than the abyss of the sea; souls pass through furnaces, and are remade by Time's hammer on the anvil of space; there are obscure crucifixions, and Last Judgments return and are re-enacted.

To Blake, the Prophetic Books were to be the new religious books of a religion which was not indeed new, for it was the 'Everlasting Gospel' of Jesus, but, because it had been seen anew by Swedenborg and by Wesley and by 'the gentle souls who guide the great wine-press of Love,' among whom was Teresa, seemed to require a new interpretation to the imagination. Blake wrote when the eighteenth century was coming to an end; he announced the new dispensation which was to come, Swedenborg had said, with the year which was the year of his birth, 1757. He looked forward steadfastly to the time when 'Sexes must vanish and cease to be,' when 'all their crimes, their punishments, their accusations of sin, all their jealousies, revenges, murders, hidings of cruelty in deceit, appear only on the outward spheres of visionary Space and Time, in the shadows of possibility by mutual forgiveness for evermore, and in the vision and the prophecy, that we may foresee and avoid the terrors of Creation and Redemption and Judgment.' He spoke to literalists, rationalists, materialists; to an age whose very infidels doubted only facts, and whose deists affirmed no more than that man was naturally religious. The rationalist's denial of everything beyond the evidence of his senses seemed to him a criminal blindness; and he has engraved a separate sheet with images and statements of the affirmation: 'There is no Natural Religion.' To Blake the literal meaning of things seemed to be of less than no importance. To worship the 'Goddess Nature' was to worship the 'God of this World,' and so to be an atheist, as even Wordsworth seemed to him to be. Religion was asleep, with Art and Literature in its arms: Blake's was the voice of the awakening angel. What he cried was that only eternal and invisible things were true, and that visible temporal things were a veil and a delusion. In this he knew himself to be on the side of Wesley and Whitefield, and that Voltaire and Rousseau, the voices of the passing age, were against him. He called them 'frozen sons of the feminine Tabernacle of Bacon, Newton, and Locke.' Wesley and Whitefield he calls the 'two servants' of God, his 'two witnesses.'

But it seemed to him that he could go deeper into the Bible than they, in their practical eagerness, had gone. 'What are the treasures of Heaven,' he asked, 'that we are to lay up for ourselves—are they any other than Mental Studies and Performances?' 'Is the Holy Ghost,' he asked, 'any other than an intellectual Fountain?' It seemed to him that he could harmonise many things once held to be discordant, and adjust the many varying interpretations of the Bible and the other books of ancient religions by a universal application of what had been taken in too personal a way. Hence many of the puzzling 'correspondences' of English cities and the tribe of Judah, of 'the Poetic Genius, which is the Lord.'

There is an outcry in *Jerusalem*:

'No individual ought to appropriate to Himself
Or to his Emanation, any of the Universal Characteristics
Of David or of Eve, of the Woman, of the Lord,
Of Reuben or of Benjamin, of Joseph or Judah or Levi.
Those who dare appropriate to themselves Universal Attributes
Are the Blasphemous Selfhoods and must be broken asunder.
A Vegetable Christ and a Virgin Eve, are the Hermaphroditic
Blasphemy: by his Maternal Birth he put off that Evil One,
And his Maternal Humanity must be put off Eternally,
Lest the Sexual Generation swallow up Regeneration:
Come, Lord Jesus, take on Thee the Satanic Body of Holiness!'

Exactly what is meant here will be seen more clearly if we compare it with a much earlier statement of the same doctrine, in the poem 'To Tirzah' in the *Songs of Experience*, and the comparison will show us all the difference between the art of Blake in 1794, and what seemed to him the needful manner of his message ten years later. 'Tirzah' is Blake's name for Natural Religion.

'Whatever is Born of Mortal Birth
Must be consumed with the Earth,
To rise from Generation free:
Then what have I to do with thee?

'The Sexes sprung from Shame and Pride
Blow'd in the morn; in evening died;
But Mercy changed Death into Sleep;
The Sexes rose to work and weep.

'Thou Mother of my Mortal part
With cruelty didst mould my Heart,
And with false, self-deceiving Tears
Didst bind my Nostrils, Eyes, and Ears;

'Didst close my Tongue in senseless clay,
And me to Mortal Life betray:
The Death of Jesus set me free:
Then what have I to do with thee?'

Here is expressed briefly and exquisitely a large part of the foundation of Blake's philosophy: that birth into the world, Christ's or ours, is a fall from eternal realities into the material affections of the senses, which are deceptions, and bind us under the bondage of nature, our 'Mother,' who is the Law; and that true life is to be regained only by the death of that self which cuts us off from our part in eternity, which we enter through the eternal reality of the imagination. In the poem, the death of Jesus symbolises that deliverance; in the passage from *Jerusalem* the Church's narrow conception of the mortal life of Jesus is rebuked, and its universal significance indicated, but in how different, how obscure, how distorted a manner. What has brought about this new manner of saying the same thing?

I think it is an endeavour to do without what had come to seem to Blake the deceiving imageries of nature, to express the truth of contraries at one and the same time, and to render spiritual realities in a literal translation. What he had been writing was poetry; now what he wrote was to be prophecy; or, as he says in *Milton*:

> 'In fury of Poetic Inspiration,
> To build the Universe Stupendous, Mental Forms Creating.'

And, seeking always the 'Minute Particulars,' he would make no compromise with earthly things, use no types of humanity, no analogies from nature; for it was against all literal acceptance of nature or the Bible or reason, of any apparent reality, that he was appealing. Hence

> 'All Human Forms identified, even Tree, Metal, Earth, and Stone, all
> Human Forms identified, living, going forth, and returning wearied
> Into the planetary lives of Years, Months, Days, and Hours.'

Hence the affirmation:

> 'For all are Men in Eternity, Rivers, Mountains, Cities, Villages';

and the voice of London saying:

> 'My Streets are my Ideas of Imagination.'

'Hence the parallels and correspondences, the names too well known to have any ready-made meaning to the emotions (London or Bath), the names so wholly unknown that they also could mean nothing to the emotions or to the memory (Bowlahoola, Golgonooza), the whole unhuman mythology, abstractions of frigid fire. In *Jerusalem* Blake interrupts himself to say:

> 'I call them by their English names; English, the rough basement.
> Los built the stubborn structure of the Language, acting against
> Albion's melancholy, who must else have been a Dumb despair.'

In the Prophetic Books we see Blake labouring upon a 'rough basement' of 'stubborn' English; is it, after all this 'consolidated and extended work,' this 'energetic exertion of his talent,' a building set up in vain, the attempt to express what must else have been, and must now for ever remain, 'a dumb despair'?

I think we must take the Prophetic Books not quite as Blake would have had us take them. He was not a systematic thinker, and he was not content to be a lyric poet. Nor indeed did he ever profess to offer us a system, built on logic and propped by reasoning, but a myth, which is a poetical creation. He said in *Jerusalem*:

> 'I must Create a System, or be enslaved by another Man's.

I will not Reason or Compare: my business is to Create.'

To Blake each new aspect of truth came as a divine gift, and between all his affirmations of truth there is no contradiction, or no other than that vital contradiction of opposites equally true. The difficulty lies in co-ordinating them into so minutely articulated a myth, and the difficulty is increased when we possess, instead of the whole body of the myth, only fragments of it. Of the myth itself it must be said that, whether from defects inherent in it or from the fragmentary state in which it comes to us, it can never mean anything wholly definite or satisfying even to those minds best prepared to receive mystical doctrine. We cannot read the Prophetic Books either for their thought only or for their beauty only. Yet we shall find in them both inspired thought and unearthly beauty. With these two things, not always found together, we must be content.

The Prophetic Books bear witness, in their own way, to that great gospel of imagination which Blake taught and exemplified. In *Jerusalem* it is stated in a single sentence: 'I know of no other Christianity and of no other Gospel than the liberty both of body and mind to exercise the Divine Arts of Imagination: Imagination, the real and eternal World of which this Vegetable Universe is but a faint shadow, and in which we shall live in our Eternal or Imaginative Bodies, when these Vegetable Mortal Bodies are no more.' 'O Human Imagination, O Divine Body I have Crucified!' he cries; and he sees continually

'Abstract Philosophy warring in enmity against Imagination,
Which is the Divine Body of the Lord Jesus, blessed for ever.'

He finds the England of his time 'generalising Art and Science till Art and Science is lost,' making

'A pretence of Art, to destroy Art, a pretence of Liberty
To destroy Liberty, a pretence of Religion to destroy Religion.'

He sees that

'The Visions of Eternity, by reason of narrowed perceptions,
Are become weak visions of Time and Space, fix'd into furrows of death.'

He sees everywhere 'the indefinite Spectre, who is the Rational Power,' crying out:

'I am God, O Sons of Men! I am your Rational Power!

Am I not Bacon and Newton and Locke who teach Humility to
Man?
Who teach Doubt and Experiment: and my two kings, Voltaire,
Rousseau.'

He sees this threefold spirit of doubt and negation overspreading the earth, 'brooding Abstract Philosophy,' destroying Imagination; and, as he looked about him,

'Every Universal Form was become barren mountains of Moral
Virtue: and every Minute Particular harden'd into grains of sand:
And all the tenderness of the soul cast forth as filth and mire.'

It is against this spiritual deadness that he brings his protest, which is to awaken Albion out of the sleep of death, 'his long and cold repose.' 'Therefore Los,' the spirit of prophecy, and thus Blake, who 'kept the Divine Vision in time of trouble,' stands in London building Golgonooza, 'the spiritual fourfold London,' the divine City of God. Of the real or earthly London he says in *Jerusalem*:

'I see London blind and age bent begging thro' the Streets
Of Babylon, led by a child, his tears run down his beard! '

Babylon, in Blake, means 'Rational Morality.' In the *Songs of Experience* we shall see the picture, at the head of the poem called 'London.' In that poem Blake numbers the cries which go up in 'London's chartered streets,' the cry of the chimneysweep, of the soldier, of the harlot; and he says:

'In every cry of every man,
In every infant's cry of fear,
In every voice, in every ban,
The mind-forged manacles I hear.'

Into these lines he condenses much of his gospel. What Blake most hated on earth were 'mind-forged manacles.' Reason seemed to him to have laid its freezing and fettering hand on every warm joy, on every natural freedom, of body and soul; all his wrath went out against the forgers and the binders of these fetters. In his earlier poems he sings the instinctive joys of innocence; in his later, the wise joys of experience; and all the Prophetic Books are so many songs of mental liberty and invectives against every form of mental oppression. 'And Jerusalem is called Liberty among the Children of Albion.' One of the Prophetic Books, *Ahania*, can be condensed into a single sentence, one of its lines: 'Truth has bounds; Error has none.' Yet this must be understood to mean that error is the 'indefinite void' and truth a thing minutely organised; not that truth can endure bondage or limitation from without. He typifies Moral Law by Rahab, the harlot of the Bible, a being of hidden, hypocritic cruelty. Chastity is no more in itself than a lure of the harlot, typifying unwilling restraint, a negation, and no personal form of energy.

'No individual can keep the Laws, for they are death
To every energy of man, and forbid the springs of life.'

It is energy that is virtue, and, above all, mental energy. 'The treasures of heaven are not negations of passion, but realities of intellect, from which all the passions emanate, uncurbed in their eternal glory.' 'It was the tree of the knowledge of good and evil that brought sin into the world by creating distinctions, by calling this good and that evil.' Blake says in *Jerusalem*:

'And in this manner of the Sons of Albion in their strength;
They take the Two Contraries which are called Qualities, with which
Every Substance is clothed, they name them Good and Evil,
From them they make an Abstract, which is a Negation
Not only of the Substance from which it is derived,
A murderer of its own Body: but also a murderer
Of every Divine Member: it is the Reasoning Power,
An Abstract objecting power, that Negatives everything.
This is the Spectre of Man: the Holy Reasoning Power,
And in its Holiness is closed the Abomination of Desolation.'

The active form of sin is judgment, intellectual cruelty, unforgivingness, punishment. 'In Hell is all self-righteousness; there is no such thing as forgiveness of sins.' In his picture of the 'Last Judgment' he represents the Furies by men, not women; and for this reason: 'The spectator may suppose them clergymen in the pulpit, scourging sin instead of forgiving it.' In *Jerusalem* he says:

'And the appearance of a Man was seen in the Furnaces,
Saving those who have sinned from the punishment of the Law
(In pity of the punisher whose state is eternal death),
And keeping them from Sin by the mild counsels of his love.'

And in his greatest paradox and deepest passion of truth, he affirms:

'I care not whether a Man is Good or Evil; all that I care
Is whether he is a Wise Man or a Fool. Go, put off Holiness
And put on Intellect.'

That holiness may be added to wisdom Blake asks only that continual forgiveness of sins which to him meant understanding, and thus intellectual sympathy; and he sees in the death of Jesus the supreme symbol of this highest mental state.

'And if God dieth not for Man and giveth not himself
Eternally for Man, Man could not exist, for Man is love,
As God is Love: every kindness to another is a little Death
In the Divine Image, nor can Man exist but by Brotherhood.'

Of Blake it may be said as he says of Albion: 'He felt that Love and Pity are the same,' and to Love and Pity he gave the ultimate jurisdiction over humanity.

Blake's gospel of forgiveness rests on a very elaborate structure, which he has built up in his doctrine of 'States.' At the head of the address to the Deists in the third chapter of *Jerusalem*, he has written: 'The Spiritual States of the Soul are all Eternal. Distinguish between the Man and his present State.' Much of his subtlest casuistry is expended on this distinction, and, as he makes it, it is profoundly suggestive. Erin says, in *Jerusalem*:

'Learn therefore, O Sisters, to distinguish the Eternal Human
That walks about among the stones of fire, in bliss and woe
Alternate, from those States or Worlds in which the Spirit travels:
This is the only means to Forgiveness of Enemies.'

The same image is used again:

'As the Pilgrim passes while the Country permanent remains,
So Men pass on; but States remain permanent for ever' ;

and, again, in almost the same words, in the prose fragment on the picture of the 'Last Judgment': 'Man passes on, but states remain for ever; he passes through them like a traveller, who may as well suppose that the places he has passed through exist no more, as a man may suppose that the states he has passed through exist no more: everything is eternal.' By states Blake means very much what we mean by moods, which, in common with many mystics, he conceives as permanent spiritual forces, through which what is transitory in man passes, while man imagines that they, more transitory than himself, are passing through him. It is from this conception of man as a traveller, and of good and evil, the passions and virtues and sensations and ideas of man, as spiritual countries, eternally remaining, through which he passes, that Blake draws his inference; condemn, if you will, the state which you call sin, but do not condemn the individual whose passage through it may be a necessity of his journey. And his litany is:

'Descend, O Lamb of God, and take away the imputation of Sin
By the creation of States and the deliverance of Individuals evermore. Amen....
Come then, O Lamb of God, and take away the remembrance of Sin.'

CHAPTER VIII

Blake had already decided to leave Felpham, 'with the full approbation of Mr. Hayley,' as early as April, 1803. 'But alas!' he writes to Butts, 'now I may say to you—what perhaps I should not dare to say to any one else—that I can alone carry on my visionary studies in London unannoyed, and that I may converse with my friends in eternity, see visions, dream dreams, and prophesy, and speak parables unobserved, and at liberty from the doubts of other mortals.' 'There is no medium or middle state,' he adds, 'and if a man is the enemy of my spiritual life while he pretends to be the friend of my corporeal, he is a real enemy.' Hayley, once fully realised, had to be shaken off, and we find Blake taking rooms on the first-floor at 17 South Molton Street, and preparing to move to London, when an incident occurs which leaves him, as he put it in a letter to Butts, 'in a bustle to defend myself against a very unwarrantable warrant from a justice of the peace in Chichester, which was taken out against me by a private in Captain Leathes' troop of 1st or Royal Dragoon Guards, for an assault and seditious words.' This was a soldier whom Blake had turned out of his garden, 'perhaps foolishly and perhaps not,' as he said, but with unquestionable vigour. 'It is certain,' he commented, 'that a too passive manner, inconsistent with my active physiognomy, had done me much mischief.' The 'contemptible business' was tried at Chichester on January 11, 1804, at the Quarter Sessions, and Blake was acquitted of the charge of high treason; 'which so gratified the auditory,' says the *Sussex Advertiser* of the date, 'that the court was, in defiance of all decency, thrown into an uproar by their noisy exultations.'

London, on his return to it, seemed to Blake as desirable as Felpham had seemed after London; and he writes to Hayley: 'The shops in London improve; everything is elegant, clean, and neat; the streets are widened where they were narrow; even Snow Hill is become almost level and is a very handsome street, and the narrow part of the Strand near St. Clement's is widened and become very elegant.' But there were other reasons for satisfaction. In a letter written before he left Felpham, Blake said: 'What is very pleasant, every one who hears of my going to London applauds it as the only course for the interest of all concerned in my works; observing that I ought not to be away from the opportunities London affords of seeing fine pictures, and the various improvements in works of art going on in London.' In October 1804 he writes to Hayley, in the most ecstatic of his letters, recording the miracle or crisis that has suddenly opened his eyes, vitalising the meditations of Felpham. 'Suddenly,' says the famous letter, 'on the day after visiting the Truchessian Gallery of pictures, I was again enlightened with the light I enjoyed in my youth, and which has for exactly twenty years been closed from me as by a door and by window-shutters. ... Dear Sir, excuse my enthusiasm, or rather madness, for I am really drunk with intellectual vision whenever I take a pencil or graver into my hand, even as I used to be in my youth, and as I have not been for twenty dark, but very profitable years.' Some of this new radiance may be seen in the watercolour of 'The River of Life,' which has been assigned by Mr. Russell to this year; and in those 'Inventions' in illustration of Blair's *Grave*, by which Blake was to make his one appeal to the public of his time.

That appeal he made through the treacherous services of a sharper named Cromek, an engraver and publisher of prints, who bought the twelve drawings for the price of twenty pounds, on the understanding that they were to be engraved by their designer; and thereupon handed them over to the fashionable Schiavonetti, telling Blake 'your drawings have had the good fortune to be engraved by one of the first artists in Europe.' He further caused a difference between Blake and Stothard which destroyed a friendship of nearly thirty years, never made up in the lifetime of either, though Blake made two efforts to be reconciled. The story of the double commission given by Cromek for a picture of Chaucer's *Canterbury Pilgrims*, and of the twofold accusation of plagiarism, is told clearly enough in the narrative of J. T. Smith, while Cunningham does his best to confuse the facts in the interests of Cromek. It has been finally summed up by Swinburne, who comes to this reasonable conclusion: 'It is probable that Stothard believed himself to be not in the wrong; it is certain that Blake was in the right.' As for Cromek, he has written himself down for all time in his true character, naked and not ashamed, in a letter to Blake of May 1807, where the false bargainer asserts: 'Herein I have been gratified; for I was determined to bring you food as well as reputation, though, from your late conduct, I have some reason to embrace your wild opinion, that to manage genius, and to cause it to produce good things, it is absolutely necessary to starve it; indeed, the opinion is considerably heightened by the recollection that your best work, the illustrations of The Grave, was produced when you and Mrs. Blake were reduced so low as to be obliged to live on half a guinea a week.' Cromek published the book by subscription in August 1808, with an 'advertisement' invoking the approval of the drawings as 'a high and original effort of genius' by eleven Royal Academicians, including Benjamin West, Flaxman, Lawrence, and Stothard. 'To the elegant and classical taste of Mr. Fuseli,' he tells us further, 'he is indebted for the excellent remarks on the moral worth and picturesque dignity of the Designs that accompany this Poem.' Fuseli praises pompously the 'genuine and unaffected attitudes,' the 'simple graces which nature and the heart alone can dictate, and only an eye inspired by both, discover,' though finding the artist 'playing on the very verge of legitimate invention.'

It is by the designs to Blair's *Grave* that Blake is still perhaps chiefly known, outside his own public; nor was he ever so clear, or, in a literal way, so convincing in his rendering of imaginative reality. Something formal tempers and makes the ecstasy explicit; the drawing is inflexibly elegant; all the Gothic secrets that had been learnt among the tombs in Westminster Abbey find their way into these stony and yet strangely living death-beds and monuments of death. No more vehement movement was ever perpetrated than that leap together of the soul and body meeting as the grave opens. If ever the soul was made credible to the mind through the eyes, it is in these designs carved out of abstract form, and planned according to a logic which is partly literal faith in imagination and partly the curtailment of scholastic drawing.

The book contains the names of more than five hundred subscribers, but only one contemporary notice has been found, a notice of two columns, mere drivel and mere raving, signed by the happily undiscovered initials R. H., in the thirty-second number of Leigh Hunt's paper, *The Examiner* (August 7, 1808, pp. 509, 510). It is under the heading 'Fine Arts,' and is called 'Blake's edition of Blair's *Grave*.' The notice is rendered specially grotesque by its serious air of arguing with what it takes to be absurdity coupled with 'an appearance of libidinousness' which 'intrudes itself upon the holiness of our thoughts and counteracts their impression.' Like most moralists of the press, this critic's meaning is hard to get at. Here, however, is a specimen: 'But a more serious censure attaches to two of these most heterogeneous and seriofantastic designs. At the awful day of judgment, before the throne of God himself, a male and female figure are described in most indecent attitudes. It is the same with the salutation of a man and his wife meeting in the pure mansions of Heaven.' Thus sanctified a voice was it that first croaked at Blake out of the 'nest of villains' which he imagined that he was afterwards to 'root out' of *The Examiner*.

A perhaps irrelevant curiosity has led many people to wonder who Blake's only critic in his lifetime, the venomous 'R. H.' of *The Examiner*, could have been. He has been run to earth: he was Robert Hunt, the brother of the editor, Leigh Hunt. I owe the record of the capture to the courtesy of Major S. Butterworth, who has copied from p. 358 of the first volume of Haydon's *Correspondence and Table-Talk* the following letter:

'4, Maida Hill West, *17th November*, 1823.

'DEAR HAYDON,

'You ask, "Am I, or was I ever, the author of any criticisms on modern works of art, signed R. H., in *The Examiner*?" and "Did I ever in my life criticise a modern picture, or influence you or your brother, Mr. Robert Hunt, directly or indirectly, to give favourable or unfavourable opinions of any modern picture or any modern artist?"

'In reply, I have to state that you certainly never wrote any articles in *The Examiner* under the signature of R. H. (which were written by my brother Robert), that you never criticised any modern picture or artist in that paper, and that you never, to my knowledge, directly or indirectly, induced any writer in *The Examiner* to give favourable or unfavourable opinions respecting works of art or their authors.

'I remain, yours truly,

'JOHN HUNT.'

Blake probably knew the name of his assailant, and probably coupled his name at once with that of his brother's, whom he took to be hiding in the same 'nest of villains.' It is only fair to suggest that, though responsible as an editor for the insertion of the articles, Leigh Hunt had nothing to do with the art criticism of his paper, which was done from the time of the second number (January 2nd, 1808) under the same signature, 'R. H.,' or occasionally, as in one of the Blake articles, without the signature, but always visibly by the same hand. The style is throughout appalling, the ideas preposterous. On November 13th of the year 1808, three months after he had written the first article on Blake, we find Robert Hunt affirming: 'As the object of our strictures on the Arts is their benefit, we will stand perpetual guard before the Temple of Genius'; and on December 3rd, 1809, three months after the second article on Blake, he reiterates, in reference to some other matter, that he 'has had no other view in this statement than the benefit o those arts of which he is enamoured, and in whose service he will always be a sincere, however feeble, volunteer.' As late as 1822 we find him offering his advice to Flaxman, who has a 'Satan overcome by St. Michael' in the Academy: We deferentially suggest to our gifted Sculptor, whether the calf of the advanced leg ought not to be a little more swelled. He mentions in passing that a picture of Turner is 'almost anything but what a picture ought to be'; and that Rembrandt is not to be compared,'in the painting of character, in which that great Painter often failed,' with our extraordinarily gifted English artist,' Mr. Rippingille, who may be remembered as a rakish improvising gentleman who used to take John Clare about the London slums. Now and then he deserts art for politics, and takes his brother's place as leader-writer. The style and the ideas do not vary, even when he writes on 'The Bill for the Bettering of the Condition of Curates,' or says of Napoleon: 'The Giant has successfully drenched his insatiable sword in the vitals of our many friends.' 'We will model from truth' may be taken as the last self-revelation of the anonymous critic who attacked Blake so venomously.

A quite different view of him is to be found in a book which was published before *The Grave* actually came out, though it contains a reference to the designs and to the 'ardent and encomiastic applause' of 'some of the first artists in the country.' The book, which contained an emblematic frontispiece designed by Blake and engraved by Cromek, was *A Father's Memoirs of his Child*, written by Benjamin Heath Malkin, then headmaster of Bury Grammar School, in which the father gives a minute and ingenuous account of his child, a prodigy of precocious intellect, who died at the age of nearly seven years. The child was accustomed to do little drawings, some of which are reproduced in the book in facsimile, and the father, after giving his own opinion of them, adds: 'Yet, as my panegyric on such a subject can carry with it no recommendation, I subjoin the testimony of Mr. Blake to this instance of peculiar ingenuity, who has given me his opinion of these various performances in the following terms:

'"They are all firm, determinate outlines, or identical form. Had the hand which executed these little ideas been that of a plagiary, who works only from the memory, we should have seen blots, called masses; blots without form, and therefore without meaning. These blots of light and dark, as being the result of labour, are always clumsy and indefinite; the effect of rubbing out and putting in, like the progress of a blind man, or of one in the dark, who feels his way, but does not see it. These are not so. Even the copy of Raphael's cartoon of St. Paul preaching is a firm, determinate outline, struck at once, as Protogenes struck his line, when he meant to make himself known to Apelles. The map of Allestone has the same character of the firm and determinate. All his efforts prove this little boy to have had that greatest of all blessings, a strong imagination, a clear idea, and a determinate vision of things in his own mind.' It is in the lengthy dedication of the book to Thomas Johnes, the translator of Froissart, that Dr. Malkin gives the very interesting personal account of Blake.

It is not certain whether Blake had ever known little Thomas Malkin, and it would be interesting to know whether it was through any actual influence of his that the child had come to his curious invention of an imaginary country. He drew the map of this country, peopled with names (Nobblede and Bobblobb, Punchpeach and Closetha) scarcely more preposterous than the names which Blake was just then discovering for his own spiritual regions, wrote its chronicles, and even made music for it. The child was born in 1795 and died in 1802, and Blake had been at Felpham since September 1800; but, if they had met before that date, there was quite time for Blake's influence to have shown itself. In 1799 the astonishing child 'could read, without hesitation, any English book. He could spell any words. ... He knew the Greek alphabet'; and on his fourth birthday, in that year, he writes to his mother saying that he has got a Latin grammar and English prints. In October 1800 he says: 'I know a deal of Latin,' and in December he is reading Burns's poems, 'which I am very fond of.' Influence or accident, the coincidence is singular, and at least shows us something in Blake's brain working like the brain of a precocious child.

In 1806 Blake wrote a generous and vigorous letter to the editor of the *Monthly Review* (July 1, 1806) in reply to a criticism which had appeared in *Bell's Weekly Messenger* on Fuseli's picture of Count Ugolino in the Royal Academy. In 1808 he had himself, and for the fifth and last time, two pictures in the Academy, and in that year he wrote the letter to Ozias Humphrey, describing one of his many 'Last Judgments,' which is given, with a few verbal errors, by J. T. Smith. In December he wrote to George Cumberland, who had written to order for a friend 'a complete set of all you have published in the way of books coloured as mine are,' that 'new varieties, or rather new pleasures, occupy my thoughts; new profits seem to arise before me so tempting that I have already involved myself in engagements that preclude all possibility of promising anything.' Does this refer to the success of Blair's *Grave*, which had just been published? He goes on: 'I have, however, the satisfaction to inform you that I have myself begun to print an account of my various inventions in Art, for which I have procured a publisher, and am determined to pursue the plan of publishing, that I may get printed without disarranging my time, which in future must alone be designing and painting.' To this project, which was never carried out, he refers again in the prospectus printed in anticipation of his exhibition, a copy of which, given to Ozias Humphreys, exists with the date May 15, 1809. A second prospectus is given by Gilchrist as follows:

'Blake's Chaucer, the Canterbury Pilgrims. This Fresco Picture, representing Chaucer's Characters, painted by William Blake, as it is now submitted to the public.

'The designer proposes to engrave in a correct and finished line manner of engraving, similar to those original copper-plates of Albert Durer, Lucas Van Leyden, Aidegrave, and the old original engravers, who were great masters in painting and designing; whose methods alone can delineate Character as it is in this Picture, where all the lineaments are distinct.

'It is hoped that the Painter will be allowed by the public (notwithstanding artfully disseminated insinuations to the contrary) to be better able than any other to keep his own characters and expressions; having had sufficient evidence in the works of our own Hogarth, that no other artist can reach the original spirit so well as the Painter himself, especially as Mr. B. is an old, well-known, and acknowledged graver.

'The size of the engraving will be three feet one inch long by one foot high. The artist engages to deliver it, finished, in one year from September next. No work of art can take longer than a year: it may be worked backwards and forwards without end, and last a man's whole life; but he will, at length, only be forced to bring it back to what it was, and it will be worse than it was at the end of the first twelve months. The value of this artist's year is the criterion of Society; and as it is valued, so does Society flourish or decay.

'The price to Subscribers, Four Guineas; two to be paid at the time of subscribing, the other two, on delivery of the print.

'Subscriptions received at No. 28, corner of Broad Street, Golden Square, where the Picture is now exhibiting, among other works, by the same artist.

'The price will be considerably raised to non-subscribers.'

The exhibition thus announced was held at the house of James Blake, and contained sixteen pictures, of which the first nine are described as 'Frescoes' or 'experiment pictures,' and the remaining seven as 'drawings,' that is, drawings in water-colour. The Catalogue (which was included in the entrance fee of half-a-crown) is Blake's most coherent work in prose, and can be read in Gilchrist, ii. 139—163. It is called 'A Descriptive Catalogue of Pictures, Poetical and Historical Inventions, painted by William Blake, in Water-Colours, being the ancient Method of Fresco Painting Restored; and Drawings, for Public Inspection, and for Sale by Private Contract.' Crabb Robinson, from whom we have the only detailed account of the exhibition, says that the pictures filled 'several rooms of an ordinary dwelling-house'. He mentions Lamb's delight in the Catalogue,[1] and his declaring 'that Blake's description was the finest criticism he had ever read of Chaucer's poem.' In that letter to Bernard Barton (May 15, 1824), which is full of vivid admiration for Blake ('I must look on him as one of the most extraordinary persons of the age'), Lamb speaks of the criticism as 'most spirited, but mystical and full of vision,' and says: 'His pictures—one in particular, the "Canterbury Pilgrims"

1. We know from Mr. Lucas's catalogue of Lamb's library that Lamb bound it up in a thic 12mo volume with his own *Confessions of a Drunkard*, Southey's *Wat Tyler*, and Lady Winchilsea's and Lord Rochester's poems.

(far above Stoth-ard's)—have great merit, but hard, dry, yet with grace.' Southey, we know from a sneer in *The Doctor* at 'that painter of great but insane genius, William Blake,' also went to the exhibition, and found, he tells us, the picture of 'The Ancient Britons,' 'one of the worst pictures, which is saying much.' A note to Mr. Swinburne's *William Blake* tells us that in the competent opinion of Mr. Seymour Kirkup this picture was 'the very noblest of all Blake's works.' It is now lost; it was probably Blake's largest work, the figures, Blake asserts, being 'full as large as life.' Of the other pictures the seventh, eighth, ninth, tenth, and sixteenth are lost; the ninth exists in a replica in 'fresco,' and the sixteenth in what is probably a first sketch.

Blake's reason for giving this exhibition was undoubtedly indignation at what he took to be Stothard's treachery in the matter of the 'Canterbury Pilgrims.' This picture (now in the National Gallery, No. 1163) had been exhibited by Cromek throughout the kingdom, and he had announced effusively, in a seven-page advertisement at the end of Blair's *Grave*, the issue of 'a print executed in the line manner of engraving, and in the same excellent style as the portrait of Mr. William Blake, prefixed to this work, by Louis Schiavonetti, Esq., V. A., the gentleman who has etched the prints that at once illustrate and embellish the present volume.' *The Descriptive Catalogue* is full of angry scorn of 'my rival,' as Blake calls Stothard, and of the 'dumb dollies' whom he has 'jumbled together' in his design, and of Hoppner for praising them in the letter quoted in the advertisement. 'If Mr. B.'s "Canterbury Pilgrims" had been done by any other power than that of the poetic visionary, it would have been as dull as his adversary's,' Blake assures us, and, no doubt, justly. The general feeling of Blake's friends, I doubt not, is summed up in an ill-spelled letter from young George Cumberland to his father, written from the Pay Office, Whitehall, October 14, 1809, which I copy in all its literal slovenliness from the letter preserved in the Cumberland Papers: 'Blakes has published a Catalogue of Pictures being the ancient method of Frescoe Painting Restored, you should tell Mr. Barry to get it, it may be the means of serving your friend. It sells for *2/6d* and may be had of J. Blake, 28 Broad St., Golden Square, at his Brothers—the Book is a great curiosity. He as given Stothard a compleet set down.'

The Catalogue is badly printed on poor paper in the form of a small octavo book of 66 pages. It is full of fierce, exuberant wisdom, which plunges from time to time into a bright, demonstrative folly; it is a confession, a criticism, and a kind of gospel of sanctity and honesty and imagination in art. The whole thing is a thinking aloud. One hears an impetuous voice as if saying: 'I have been scorned long enough by these fellows, who owe to me all that they possess; it shall be so no longer.' As he thinks, his pen follows; he argues with foes actually visible to him; never does he realise the indifferent public that may glance at what he has written, and how best to interest or convince it if it does. He throws down a challenge, and awaits an answer.

What answer came is rememberable among the infamies of journalism. Only one newspaper noticed the exhibition, and this was again *The Examiner*. The notice appeared under the title 'Mr. Blake's Exhibition' in No. 90, September 17, 1809, pp. 605-6, where it fills two columns. It is unsigned, but there can be no doubt that it was written by the R. H. of the former article. The main part of it is taken up by extracts from the *Descriptive Catalogue*, italicized and put into small capitals 'to amuse the reader, and satisfy him of the truth of the foregoing remarks.' This is all that need be quoted of the foregoing remarks:

'But when the ebullitions of a distempered brain are mistaken for the sallies of genius by those whose works have exhibited the soundest thinking in art, the malady has indeed attained a pernicious height, and it becomes a duty to endeavour to arrest its progress. Such is the case with the productions and admirers of William Blake, an unfortunate lunatic, whose personal inoffensiveness secures him from confinement, and, consequently, of whom no public notice would have been taken, if he was not forced on the notice and animadversion of *The Examiner*, in having been held up to public admiration by many esteemed amateurs and professors as a genius in some respect original and legitimate. The praises which these gentlemen bestowed last year on this unfortunate man's illustrations to Blair's *Grave* have, in feeding his vanity, stimulated him to publish his madness more largely, and thus again exposed him, if not to the derision, at least to the pity of the public. ... Thus encouraged, the poor man fancies himself a great master, and has painted a few wretched pictures, some of which are unintelligible allegory, others an attempt at sober character by caricature representation, and the whole "blotted and blurred," and very badly drawn. These he calls an Exhibition, of which he has published a Catalogue, or rather a farrago of nonsense, unintelligibleness, and egregious vanity, the wild effusions of a distempered brain. One of the pictures represents Chaucer's Pilgrims, and is in every respect a striking contrast to the admirable picture of the same subject by Mr. Stothard, from which an exquisite print is forthcoming from the hand of Schiavon-etti.'

The last great words of the Catalogue, 'If a man is master of his profession, he cannot be ignorant that he is so; and, if he is not employed by those who pretend to encourage art, he will employ himself, and laugh in secret at the pretences of the ignorant, while he has every night dropped into his shoe, as soon as he puts it off, and puts out the candle, and gets into bed, a reward for the labours of the day such as the world cannot give, and patience and time await to give him all that the world can give': those noble, lovely, pathetic and prophetic words, are quoted at the end of the article without comment, as if to quote them was enough. It was.

In 1803 William Blake sold to Thomas Butts eleven drawings for fourteen guineas. In 1903 twelve water-colour drawings in illustration of *L'Allegro* and *Il Penseroso* were sold for £1,960, and the twenty-one water-colour drawings for Job for £5,600. These figures have their significance, but the significance must not be taken to mean any improvement in individual taste. When a selection from the pictures in the Butts collection was on view at Sotheby's I heard a vulgar person with a loud voice, a dealer or a dealer's assistant, say with a guffaw: 'It would make me sick to have these things round my room.' That vulgar person represents the eternal taste of the multitude; only, in the course of a hundred years, a few men of genius have repeated after one another that Blake was a man of genius, and their united voices have carried further than the guffaws of vulgar persons, repeated generation after generation. And so in due course, when Blake has been properly dead long enough, there is a little public which, bidding against itself, gambles cheerfully for the possession of the scraps of paper on which he sent in his account, against the taste of his age and the taste of all the ages.

Blake himself had never any doubt of his own greatness as an artist, and some of the proud or petulant things which he occasionally wrote (the only outbreaks of impatience in a life wholly given up to unceasing and apparently unrewarded labour) have been quoted against him as petty or unworthy, partly because they are so uncalculated and so childlike. Blake 'bore witness,' as he might have said, that he had done his duty: 'for that I cannot live without doing my duty, to lay up treasures in heaven, is certain and determined,' he writes from Felpham. And he asserted the truth of his own genius, its truth in the spiritual sense, its divine origin, as directly and as emphatically as he asserted everything which he had apprehended as truth. He is merely stating what seems to him an obvious but overlooked fact when he says: 'In Mr. B.'s Britons the blood is seen to circulate in their limbs: he defies competition in colouring'; and again: 'I am, like other men, just equal in invention and execution of my work.' All art, he had realised, which is true art, is equal, as every diamond is a diamond. There is only true and false art. Thus when he says in his prospectus of 1793 that he has been 'enabled to bring before the Public works (he is not afraid to say) of equal magnitude and consequence with the productions of any age or country,' he means neither more nor less than when he says in the *Descriptive Catalogue* of 1809: 'He knows that what he does is not inferior to the grandest antiques. Superior it cannot be, for human power cannot go beyond either what he does or what they have done; it is the gift of God, it is inspiration and vision..... The human mind cannot go beyond the gift of God, the Holy Ghost.' It is in humility rather than in pride that he equals himself with those who seemed to him the genuine artists, the humility of a belief that all art is only a portion of that 'Poetic Genius, which is the Lord,' offered up in homage by man, and returning, in mere gratitude, to its origin. When he says, 'I do not pretend to paint better than Rafael or Michael Angelo, or Julio Romano, or Albert Durer, but I do pretend to paint finer than Rubens, or Rembrandt, or Titian, or Correggio,' he merely means, in that odd coupling and contrasting of names, to assert his belief in the supremacy of strong, clear, masculine execution over what seemed to him (to his limited knowledge, not false instinct) the heresy and deceit of 'soft and effeminate' execution, the 'broken lines, broken masses, and broken colours' of the art which 'loses form.' In standing up for his ideal of art, he stands up himself, like a champion. 'I am hid,' he writes on the flyleaf of *Reynolds's Discourses*, and, in the last sentence of that 'Public Address' which was never printed, he declares: 'Resentment for personal injuries has had some share in this public address, but love to my art, and zeal for my country, a much greater.' And in the last sentence of the *Descriptive Catalogue*, he sums up the whole matter, so far as it concerned him, finally, and with a 'sure and certain hope' which, now that it has been realised, so long afterwards, comes to us like a reproach.

'Shall Painting,' asks Blake in his *Descriptive Catalogue*, 'be confined to the sordid drudgery of facsimile representations of merely mortal and perishing substances, and not be, as poetry and music are, elevated into its own proper sphere of invention and visionary conception? No, it shall not be so! Painting, as well as poetry and music, exists and exults in immortal thoughts.' It was to restore this conception of art to England that Blake devoted his life. 'The Enquiry in England,' he said, in his marginalia to Reynolds, 'is not whether a Man has Talents and Genius, but whether he is Passive and Polite and a Virtuous Ass.' He says there: 'Ages are all Equal, but Genius is always above the Age.' He looks on Bacon and Locke and Burke and Reynolds as men who 'mock Inspiration and Vision.' 'Inspiration and Vision,' he says, 'was then, and now is, and I hope will always Remain, my Element, my Eternal Dwelling-place.' 'The Ancients did not mean to Impose when they affirmed their belief in Vision and Revelation. Plato was in Earnest Milton was in Earnest. They believed that God did visit Man Really and Truly.' Further, 'Knowledge of Ideal Beauty is not to be Acquired. It is born with us.... Man is Born Like a Garden ready Planted and Sown. This World is too poor to produce one Seed.'

What Blake meant by vision, how significantly yet cautiously he interchanged the words 'seen' and 'imagined,' has been already noted in that passage of the *Descriptive Catalogue*, where he answers his objectors: 'The connoisseurs and artists who have made objections to Mr. B.'s mode of representing spirits with real bodies would do well to consider that the Venus, the Minerva, the Jupiter, the Apollo, which they admire in Greek statues are, all of them, representations of spiritual existences, of Gods immortal, to the ordinary perishing organ of sight; and yet they are embodied and organised in solid marble. Mr. B. requires the same latitude, and all is well.' Then comes the great definition, which I will not repeat: 'He who does not imagine in stronger and better lineaments.'

'The world of imagination,' he says elsewhere, 'is infinite and eternal, whereas the world of generation or vegetation is finite and temporal. There exist in that eternal world the eternal realities of everything which we see reflected in this vegetable glass of nature.' What is said here, transmuted by an instinct wholly an artist's into a great defence of the reality of imagination in art, is a form of the central doctrine of the mystics, formulated by Swedenborg in something very like Blake's language, though with errors or hesitations which is what Blake sets himself to point out in his marginalia to Swedenborg. As, in those marginalia, we see Blake altering every allusion to God into an allusion to 'the Poetic Genius,' so, always, we shall find him understanding every promise of Christ, or Old Testament prophecy, as equally translatable into terms of the imaginative life, into terms of painting, poetry, or music. In the rendering of vision he required above all things that fidelity which can only be obtained through 'minutely particular' execution. 'Invention depends Altogether upon Execution or Organisation; as that is right or wrong, so is the Invention perfect or imperfect. Whoever is set to Undermine the Execution of Art is set to destroy Art. Michael Angelo's Art depends on Michael Angelo's Execution Altogether. . . . He who admires Rafael Must admire Rafael's Execution. He who does not admire Rafael's Execution can not admire Rafael.' Finally, 'the great and golden rule of art as well as of life,' he says in the *Descriptive Catalogue*, 'is this: that the more distinct, sharp, and wiry the bounding line, the more perfect the work of art; and the less keen and sharp, the greater is the evidence of weak imagination, plagiarism, and bungling. . . . What is it that distinguishes honesty from knavery, but the hard and wiry line of rectitude and certainty in the actions and intentions? Leave out this line, and you leave out life itself. All is chance again, and the line of the Almighty must be drawn out upon it again, before man or beast can exist.'

In *Har and Heva bathing* there is the smooth effect of a mezzotint—large, smooth, smiling forms, with strangely staring eyes, with gliding naively surreptitious movements—a vast length, delicate finish—yet with all this a certain enigmatic grace. The *Ascension*, a water-colour, has primitive blues and the rising figure of the Saviour; there are two angels curving in descent by his side; below are the eleven rigid figures and staring heads and raised and clasped hands of the Disciples—all the soul in their eyes.

There is another drawing slightly touched with colour, of dead bodies in a corner of ruined walls on which a vulture perches with open beak; beyond, a woman searches in a field; close to, other women bend and embrace dead faces in armour; a young man and an old man look down on the dead with terror and dismay. In another, a vague and sinister and terrible atmosphere of disaster, intense with heat, intense with suspense, exhales a not too precise effect of strange horror which invades the senses like an opium dream. In another, coloured prettily with Stothard's colour, solid angels with flower-baskets and harps (there is also a horse and rider) scatter dreams, perhaps, on a woman who lies asleep. To this might be applied Ruskin's sentence in *Modern Painters* 'slurred or soft lines (always the sign of vice in art).' There is something splendid in *Moses displaying the Tablets of the Law*, a pen-and-ink drawing – an embodied gesture, hardly more than a gesture of authority.

Among Blake's wonderful colour-prints, is *Nebuchadnezzar*, which represents him crawling on all fours in his shaggy insanity; the tawny beard trails across the left hand; the nails are literally like bird s claws, the flesh tints are very red; the glaring eyes have almost lost their human character; the background represents a thick jungle. Take for instance, the idea of Beauty. Almost every one can see the beauty of Raphael, only a certain number can see the beauty of Velasquez, not many can see the beauty of Blake. In the human figure, every one can see the beauty of a breast; not many can see the beauty of a shoulder- blade, such as one finds in Degas, in whose astonishing drawings from the nude he has made woman the animal; woman, in a strange sense, the Idol. In his drawings there is always a certain luxury. In Rodin luxury becomes geometrical: its axioms are demonstrated algebraically. In nature, every one can see the beauty of the Alps at dawn; not many can see beauty of a putrescent pool. Yet all these are but different forms of the same essential beauty; all wait patiently for the same acceptance, all offer themselves to the same mere sight of the eyes.

Lamech and his two Wives represents Lamech looking with horrid remorse on the young man he has slain; his wives, beautifully grouped, cling together in dismay. There is a great effect of dark sky and hills, their edges dimly defined in glimmering light. In *Elijah* mounted in the Fiery Chariot, he lays hold of the reins with his right hand; he is draped—but Elisha, who stands before him, is perfectly naked and looks as ancient as Elijah. The horses are as it were of fire compact; fire flows out in place of chariot wheels; behind Elijah is a sphere of rolling red flames; there is a blaze of yellow in the sky. The colours of this Promethean creation are austerely luminous and very solid. *The Good and Evil Angels struggling for the possession of a child* represents the good angel holding the child — the Evil One enveloped in flames, seeks to seize him.

There are three of Blake's colour-prints that represent *Satan exulting over Eve*. In one, Satan is seen as a Toad, haunting Eve's dreams; Adam and Eve lie on a natural carpet of leaves; around them a mass of rounded forms, simulating shut roses; two angels float above them, with small javelins. In the next Satan turns towards the left; the flesh is almost colourless, and on the whole sensuous.The Serpent, with a comb of fire,'in his own volumes inter-volved,' glides away from their feet. In the third, which is magnificent, Satan, above the scented bower under which Eve and Adam are seated, holds the Serpent—an amazingly subtle, prismatic-hued Serpent—which seems to drain his vitals. The sun sets to the right; the moon and the stars are visible in the dark sky.

One of his coloured designs for *Paradise Lost, Eve eating the forbidden fruit.*, is wonderful; she eats the apple out of the serpent's jaws; other fruits hang from the brambles, that glow in the sun's heat. The tree's trunk is cramped with enormous parasites, which, as if they were the roots of the tree itself, reach down along the ground. On her left stands Adam, unconscious of the beginning of all Evil, of its origin, from the Serpent's temptation of the first Created Woman. Menacing and lurid lightning flashes between them—a stormy sky blackens in the dark distance — and the lightnings that flash around Adam are less angry in colour. All these, which have an ordered tumultuous decoration and which stamp an image, have that strange unreality which is more real than eyes can see. The Serpent who embraces Eve and lays his flattened head on her breast with such conquering weight, is part of a decoration of splendid certainty.

Much of Blake's abnormality is seen in the menstrual suns of his designs, the two colours, shadowed darker, ring within ring. The beginning of this conception might be found in one of his designs where Woman finds her child, sprung of the earth in the fashion of a mandrake, which, were she to pluck it, she must certainly go mad; its leaves are poisonous, it bears no fruit, yet it has something of the serpent's wisdom. In another the same woman wrenches her naked child out of the earth's dust, that shrieks as the rent earth shrieks; unaware, one imagines, that the seal of her own death, as well as her child's, must surely come upon her from the uprooting of the mandrake. She is seen again, with knees drawn up and hooded head, a worm-like woman; the adder lifts his venomous head behind her; she endures the plague of her inevitable death: sentient wings of the winds converge from the four quarters of the world, the void is rent violently asunder.

Certainly, in these two sentences in *The Marriage of Heaven and Hell,* Blake reveals, in tragic hints, among his monstrous conceptions, such as the one I have referred to, one of his divine doctrines. 'By degrees we behold the infinite abyss, fiery with smoke of a burning city; beneath us at an immense distance was the sun, black but shining; round it were fiery tracks on which revolved vast spiders, crawling after their prey - which flew or rather swam in the infinite deep, in the most terrific shapes of animals sprung from corruption, and the air was full of them, and seemed composed of them; these are Devils, and are called Powers of the Air. I now asked my companion which was my eternal lot? He said, Between the black and white spiders.'

Rossetti, in his Notes on Blake wrote: 'In each style of the art of the period, and more especially in the poetic style, there is often some one central initiatory man, to whom personally, if not to the care of the world, it is important that his creative power should be held to be his own, and that his ideas and slowly perfected materials should not be caught up before he had them ready for his own use. Yet, consciously or unconsciously, such an one's treasures and possessions are, time after time, while he still lives and needs them, sent forth to the world by others in forms from which he cannot perhaps again clearly claim what is his own, but which render the material useless to him henceforward. Hardly wonderful, after all, if for once an impetuous man of this kind is found raising the hue and cry, careless whether people heed him or no. It is no small provocation, be sure, when the gazers hoot you as outstripped in your race, and you know all the time that the man ahead, whom they shout for, is only a flying thief.'

A painter of souls, like Blake, must always obtain a large part of the admiration, or the forgiveness, which we extend to him, by his technical skill, in the treatment of material to which success is impossible. The direst representation of anything unseen by the eyes, and only mediately conceived by the imagination, can only affect us in the way intended by the artist if it makes its appeal to us by its qualities of beautiful line, beautiful colour, or beauty of composition. Blake, at his best, is so tremendous, because in his endeavour to give form to the morning stars singing together, and God riding on the whirlwind, and the worms talking to one another on the earth, he creates life, and the movement of figures, and the passion of gesture, with so unwearied an energy. Where the line is poor, the conception dwindles; no profound meaning was ever conveyed in pictorial art except through sureness of hand, through a technique definitely excellent in its own way. The mistake of those who have praised such a painter for his conceptions, and condemned him for his technique, lies in a confusion between what is artistically right, that is, truthful to beauty, and what is academically correct, that is faithful to rule. God's arm, in the drawing at the beginning *of Europe,* is out of all human proportion, in a figure done after the ordinary type of humanity; but the arm is technically superb, because it expresses the instant energy of Omnipotence, not to the mind, but to the mind through the eye, unhesitatingly. Poor technique would have been to draw a faultlessly modelled arm, and to have left mind and eye uninterested and unconvinced. But there are painters who are not painters of souls, like Blake, but painters of dreams and the brooding imagery of the senses, like Rossetti; and these, too, are able to bring us under the subtlety of their mesmerism only by their masterly obedience to technique, not by their disregard of it. Rossetti had never any great command over his material, but his pictures are good or bad just in proportion as he admitted or refused to admit the limits of pictorial expression, and the degree to which idea or sensation can be symbolized in form, of which the idea or sensation is only a passing guest. As his intentions overcome him, as he becomes the slave and no longer the master of his dreams, his pictures become no longer symbols, but idols. Venus, growing more and more Asiatic as the mooned crescent begins to glimmer above her head, and her name changes from Aphrodite into Astarte, loses all the freshness of the waves from which she was born, and her own sorcery hardens her into a wooden image painted for savage worship. Dreams are no longer content to be turned into waking realities, taking the colour of the daylight, that they may be visible to our eyes; but they remain lunar, spectral, an unintelligible menace.

In Blake's work a great fundamental conception is rarely lacking, and the conception is not, as it has often been asserted, a literary, but always a pictorial, one. At times imagination and execution are wholly untired, as in the splendid water-colour of 'Death on the Pale Horse,' in which not only every line and colour is alive with passionate idea, the implacable and eternal joy of destruction, but also with a realized beauty, a fully grasped invention. No detail has been slurred in vision, or in the setting down of the vision: the crowned old man with the sword, the galloping horse, the pestilential figure of putrid scales and flames below, and the wide-armed angel with the scroll above. In the vision of 'Fire' there is grandeur and, along with it, something inadequately seen, inadequately rendered. Flame and smoke embrace, coil, spire, swell in bellying clouds, divide into lacerating tongues, tangle and whirl ecstatically upward and onward, like a venomous joy in action, painting the air with all the colour of all the flowers of evil. But the figures in the foreground are partly Academic studies, partly archaic dolls, in which only the intention is admirable. In 'Job Confessing his Presumption to God' one sees all that is great and all that is childish in Blake's genius. I have never seen so sufficing a suggestion of disembodied divine forces as in this whirling cloud of angels, cast out and swept round by the wind of God's speed, like a cascade of veined and tapering wings, out of which ecstatic and astonished heads leap forward. But in the midst of the wheel a fierce old man, with outstretched arms (who is an image of God certainly not corrected out of any authentic vision), and, below, the extinguished figure of Job's friends, and Job, himself one of Blake's gnome-like old men with a face of rigid awe and pointing fingers of inarticulate terror, remain no more than statements, literal statements, of the facts of the imagination. They are summarised remembrances of vision, not anything 'imagined in stronger and better lineaments, and in stronger and better light, than the perishing mortal eye can see.'

Or, might it not be said that it is precisely through this minute accuracy to the detail of imagination that this visionary reality comes to seem to us unreal? In Blake every detail is seen with intensity, and with equal intensity. No one detail is subordinated to another, every inch of his surface is equally important to him; and from this unslackening emphasis come alike his arresting power and the defect which leaves us, though arrested, often unconvinced. In his most splendid things, as in 'Satan exulting over Job' and 'Cain fleeing from the Grave of Abel,' which are painted on wood, as if carved or graved, with a tumult of decorative colour, detail literally overpowers the sense of sight, like strong sunlight, and every outline seizes and enters into you simultaneously. At times, as in 'The Bard of Gray,' and 'The

Spiritual Form of Pitt' in the National Gallery, he is mysteriously lyrical in his paint, and creates a vague emotion out of a kind of musical colour, which is content to suggest. Still more rarely, as in the ripe and admirable 'Canterbury Pilgrims,' which is a picture in narrative, as like Chaucer as Chaucer himself, but unlike any other picture, he gives us a vision of worldly reality; but it was of this picture that he said: 'If Mr. B.'s "Canterbury Pilgrims" had been done by any other power than that of the poetic visionary, it would have been as dull as his adversary's.' Pure beauty and pure terror creep and flicker in and out of all his pictures, with a child's innocence; and he is unconscious of how far he is helped or hindered, as an artist, by that burden of a divine message which is continually upon him. He is unconscious that with one artist the imagination may overpower the technique, as awe overpowers the senses, while to another artist the imagination gives new life to the technique. Blake did not understand Rembrandt, and imagined that he hated him; but there are a few of his pictures in which Rembrandt is strangely suggested. In 'The Adoration of the Three Kings' and in 'The Angel appearing to Zacharias' there is a lovely depth of colour, bright in dimness, which has something of the warmth and mystery of Rembrandt, and there are details in the design of 'The Three Kings' (the door open on the pointing star in the sky and on the shadowy multitude below) which are as fine in conception as anything in the Munich 'Adoration of the Shepherds.' But in these, or in the almost finer 'Christ in the Garden, sustained by an Angel' (fire flames about the descending angel, and the garden is a forest of the night), how fatal to our enjoyment is the thought of Rembrandt! To Rembrandt, too, all things were visions, but they were visions that he saw with unflinching eyes; he saw them with his hands; he saw them with the faces and forms of men, and with the lines of earthly habitations.

And, above all, Rembrandt, all the greatest painters, saw a picture as a whole, composed every picture consciously, giving it unity by his way of arranging what he saw. Blake was too humble towards vision to allow himself to compose or arrange what he saw, and he saw in detail, with an unparalleled fixity and clearness. Every picture of Blake, quite apart from its meaning to the intelligence, is built up in detail like a piece of decoration; and, widely remote as are both intention and result, I am inclined to think he composed as Japanese artists compose, bit by bit, as he saw his picture come piece by piece before him. In every picture there is a mental idea, and there is also a pictorial conception, working visually and apart from the mental idea. In the greatest pictures (in the tremendous invention, for instance, of the soldiers on Calvary casting lots for the garments of Christ), the two are fused, with overwhelming effect; but it happens frequently that the two fail to unite, and we see the picture, and also the idea, but not the idea embodied in the picture.

Blake's passion for detail, and his refusal to subordinate any detail for any purpose, is to be seen in all his figures, of which the bodies seem to be copied from living statues, and in which the faces are wrung into masks of moods which they are too urgent to interpret. A world of conventional patterns, in which all natural things are artificial and yet expressive, is peopled by giants and dolls, muscular and foolish, in whom strength becomes an insane gesture and beauty a formal prettiness. Not a flower or beast has reality, as our eyes see it, yet every flower and beast is informed by an almost human soul, not the mere vitality of animal or vegetable, but a consciousness of its own lovely or evil shape. His snakes are not only wonderful in their coils and colours, but each has his individual soul, visible in his eyes, and interpreting those coils and colours. And every leaf, unnatural yet alive, and always a piece of decoration, peers with some meaning of its own out of every corner, not content to be forgotten, and so uneasily alive that it draws the eye to follow it. 'As poetry,' he said, 'admits not a letter that is insignificant, so painting admits not a grain of sand or a blade of grass insignificant—much less an insignificant blur or mark.' The stones with which Achan has been martyred live each with a separate and evil life of its own, not less vivid and violent than the clenched hands raised to hurl other stones; there is menacing gesture in the cloud of dust that rises behind them. And these human beings and these angels, and God (sometimes an old bowed Jew, fitted into a square or lozenge of winged heads) are full of the energy of a life which is betrayed by their bodies. Sometimes they are mere child's toys, like a Lucifer of bright baubles, painted chromatically, with pink hair and blushing wings, hung with bursting stars that spill out animalculas. Sometimes the whole man is a gesture and convulses the sky; or he runs, and the earth vanishes under him. But the gesture devours the man also; his force as a cipher annihilates his very being.

In greatness of conception Blake must be compared with the greatest among artists, but the difference between Blake and Michelangelo is the difference between the artist in whom imagination overpowers technique, as awe overpowers the senses, and the artist in whom imagination gives new life to technique. No one, as we have seen, was more conscious of the identity which exists in the work of the greatest artists between conception and execution. But in speaking of invention and execution as equal, he is assuming, as he came to do, the identity of art and inspiration, the sufficiency of first thoughts in art. 'Be assured,' he writes to Mr. Butts from Felpham, 'that there is not one touch in those drawings and pictures but what came from my head and heart in unison..... If I were to do them over again, they would lose as much as they gained, because they were done in the heat of my spirit.' He was an inexhaustible fountain of first thoughts, and to him first thoughts only were of importance. The one draughtsman of the soul, he drew, no doubt, what he saw as he saw it; but he lacked the patience which is a part of all supreme genius. Having seen his vision, he is in haste to record what he has seen hastily; and he leaves the first rough draft as it stands, not correcting it by a deliberate seeing over again from the beginning, and a scrupulous translation of the terms of eternity into the terms of time. I was once showing Rodin some facsimiles of Blake's drawings, and telling him about Blake, I said: 'He used to literally see these figures; they are not mere inventions,' 'Yes,' said Rodin, 'he saw them once; he should have seen them three or four times.' There, it seems to me, is the fundamental truth about the art of Blake: it is a record of vision which has not been thoroughly mastered even as vision. 'No man,' said Blake, 'can improve an original invention; nor can an original invention exist without execution organised, delineated, and articulated, either by God or man.' And he said also: 'He who does not imagine in stronger and better lineaments, and in stronger and better light, than his perishing mortal eye can see, does not imagine at all.' But Blake's imagination is in rebellion, not only against the limits of reality, but against the only means by which he can make vision visible to others. And thus he allows himself to be mastered by that against which he rebels: that power of the hand by which art begins where vision leaves off.

CHAPTER IX

Nothing is known of Blake's life between 1809, the date of his exhibition, and 1818, when he met the chief friend and helper of his later years, John Linnell. Everything leads us to believe that those nine years were years of poverty and neglect. Between 1815 and 1817 we find him doing engraver's task-work for Flaxman's *Hesiod*, and for articles, probably written by Flaxman, on Armour and Sculpture in Rees's *Encyclopaedia*. Gilchrist tells a story, on the authority of Tatham, of Blake copying the cast of the Laocoon among the students at the Royal Academy, and of Fuseli, then the keeper, coming up with the just and pleasant remark that it was they who should learn of him, not he of them. The *Milton* and the *Jerusalem*, both dated 1804, were printed at some time during this period. Gilchrist suggests that the reason why Blake issued no more engraved books from his press was probably his inability to pay for the copper required in engraving; and his suggestion is confirmed in a letter to Dawson Turner, a Norfolk antiquary, dated June 9, 1818, a few days before the meeting with Linnell. Blake writes: 'I send you a list of the different works you have done me the honour to inquire after. They are unprofitable enough to me, though expensive to the buyer. Those I printed for Mr. Humphry are a selection from the different books of such as could be printed without the writing, though to the loss of some of the best things; for they, when printed perfect, accompany poetical personifications and acts, without which poems they never could have been executed:

	£	s.	d.
America, 18 prints folio,	5	5	0
Europe, 17 do. do.,	5	5	0
Visions, 8 do. do.,	3	3	0
Thel, 6 do. quarto,	2	2	0
Songs of Innocence, 28 prints octavo,	3	3	0
Songs of Experience, 26 do. octavo,	3	3	0

Urizen, 28 prints quarto,	5	5	0
Milton, 50 do. do.,	10	10	0
12 large prints, size of each about 2 ft. by 1½ ft., historical and poetical, printed in colours, each	5	5	0

The last twelve prints are unaccompanied by any writing. The few I have printed and sold are sufficient to have gained me great reputation as an artist, which was the chief thing intended. But I have never been able to produce a sufficient number for general sale by means of a regular publisher. It is therefore necessary to me that any person wishing to have any or all of them should send me their order to print them on the above terms, and I will take care that they shall be done at least as well as any I have yet produced.'

If we compare this list with the printed list of twenty-five years back (see p. 50) we shall see that the prices are now half as many guineas as they were once shillings; in a letter to Cumberland, nine years later, they have gone up by one, two, or three guineas apiece, and Blake tells Cumberland that 'having none remaining of all that I had printed, I cannot print more except at a great loss. For at the time I printed these things I had a little house to range in. Now I am shut up in a corner, therefore I am forced to ask a price for them that I can scarce expect to get from a stranger. I am now printing a set of the *Songs of Innocence and Experience* for a friend at ten guineas, which I cannot do under six months consistent with my other work, so that I have little hope of doing any more of such things. The last work is a poem entitled *Jerusalem, the Emanation of the Giant Albion*, but find that to print it will cost my time to the value of twenty guineas. One I have finished. It contains 100 plates, but it is not likely that I shall get a customer for it.'[1]

Gilchrist tells us, by an error which was pointed out in the life of Palmer by his son, in 1892, that Blake met Linnell in 1813. It was in 1818, and the first entry relating to Blake in Linnell's journal is dated June 24. In a letter communicated to me by Mr. Sampson, Mr. John Linnell, junior, states that his father took in October or November 1817 the greater part of a house at 38 Rathbone Place, where he lived till the end of 1818; he then took a house at

1. I take the text of this letter, not from Mr. Russell's edition, but from the fuller text printed by Mr. Ellis in *The Real Blake*.

Cirencester Place, Fitzroy Square. Mr. Linnell gives the following extract from his father's autobiographical notes: 'At Rathbone Place, 1818 ... here I first became acquainted with William Blake, to whom I paid a visit in company with the younger Mr. Cumberland. Blake lived then in South Molton Street, Oxford Street, second floor. We soon became intimate, and I employed him to help me with an engraving of my portrait of Mr. Upton, a Baptist preacher, which he was glad to do, having scarcely enough employment to live by at the prices he could obtain; everything in Art was at a low ebb then..... I soon encountered Blake's peculiarities, and somewhat taken aback by the boldness of some of his assertions, I never saw anything the least like madness, for I never opposed him spitefully, as many did, but being really anxious to fathom, if possible, the amount of truth which might be in his most startling assertions, generally met with a sufficiently rational explanation in the most really friendly and conciliatory tone.'

From 1818 Linnell became, in his own independent way, the chief friend and disciple of Blake. Himself a man of narrow but strong individuality, he realized and accepted Blake for what he was, worked with him and for him, introduced him to rich and appreciative buyers like Sir Thomas Lawrence, and gave him, out of his own carefully controlled purse, a steady price for his work, which was at least enough for Blake to live on. There are notes in his journal of visits to picture-galleries together; to the Academy, the British Gallery, the Water-Colour Exhibition, the Spring Gardens Exhibition; 'went with Mr. B. to see Harlow's copy of the Transfiguration' (August 20, 1819), 'went with Mr. Blake to British Museum to see prints' (April 4 and 24, 1823). In 1820 there are notes of two visits to Drury Lane Theatre. It was probably early in 1819 that Linnell introduced Blake to his friend John Varley, the water-colour painter and astrologer, for whom Blake did the famous 'visionary heads.' A vivid sketch of the two arguing, drawn by Linnell, is given in Mr. Story's Life of Linnell. Varley, though an astrologer on the mathematical side, was no visionary. He persuaded Blake to do a series of drawings, naming historical or legendary people to him, and carefully writing down name and date of the imaginary portraits which Blake willingly drew, and believing, it has been said, in the reality of Blake's visions more than Blake himself. Cunningham, in his farcical way, tells the story as he may have got it from Varley, for he claims in a letter to Linnell to have 'received much valuable information from him.' But the process has been described, more simply, by Varley himself in his *Treatise of Zodiacal Physiognomy* (1828), where the 'Ghost of a Flea' and the 'Constellation Cancer' are reproduced in engraving. Some of the heads are finely symbolical, and I should have thought the ghost of a flea, in the sketch, an invention more wholly outside nature if I had not seen, in Rome and in London, a man in whom it is impossible not to recognise the type, modified to humanity, but scarcely by a longer distance than the men from the animals in Giovanni della Porta's 'Fisonomia dell' Huomo.'

It was in 1820, the year in which Blake began his vast picture of the 'Last Judgment,' only finished in the year of his death, that he did the seventeen woodcuts to Thornton's *Virgil*, certainly one of his greatest, his most wholly successful achievements. The book was for boys' schools, and we find Blake returning without an effort to the childlike mood of the *Songs of Innocence and Experience*. The woodcuts have all the natural joy of those early designs, an equal simplicity, but with what added depth, what richness, what passionate strength! Blake was now engraving on wood for the first time, and he had to invent his own way of working. Just what he did has never been better defined than in an article which appeared in the *Athenaum* of January 21, 1843, one of the very few intelligent references to Blake which can be found in print between the time of his death and the date of Gilchrist's *Life*. 'We hold it impossible,' says the writer, 'to get a genuine work of art, unless it come pure and unadulterated from the mind that conceived it.... Still more strongly is the author's meaning marked in the few wood-engravings which that wonderful man Blake cut himself for an edition of Thornton's *Pastorals of Virgil*. In token of our faith in the principle here announced, we have obtained the loan of one of Blake's original blocks, from Mr. Linnell, who possesses the whole series, to print, as an illustration of our argument, that, amid all drawbacks, there exists a power in the work of the man of genius, which no one but himself can utter fully. Side by side we have printed a copy of an engraver's improved version of the same subject. When Blake had produced his cuts, which were, however, printed with an apology, a shout of derision was raised by the wood-engravers. "This will never do!" said they; "we will show what it ought to be"—that is, what the public taste would like—and they produced the above amendment! The engravers were quite right in their estimate of public taste; and we dare say many will agree with them even now: yet, to our minds, Blake's rude work, utterly without pretension, too, as an engraving—the merest attempt of a fresh apprentice—is a work of genius; whilst the latter is but a piece of smooth, tame mechanism.'

Blake lived at South Molton Street for seventeen years. In 1821, 'on his landlord's leaving off business, and retiring to France,' says Linnell, he removed to Fountain Court, in the Strand, where he took the first floor of 'a private house kept by Mr. Banes, whose wife was a sister of Mrs. Blake.' Linnell tells us that he was at this time 'in want of employment,' and, he says, 'before I knew his distress he had sold all his collection of old prints to Messrs. Colnagi and Co.' Through Linnell's efforts, a donation of £25 was about the same time sent to him from the Royal Academy.

Fountain Court (the name is still perpetuated on a metal slab) was called so until 1883, when the name was changed to Southampton Buildings. It has all been pulled down and rebuilt, but I remember it fifteen years ago, when there were lodging-houses in it, by the side of the stage-door of Terry's Theatre. It was a narrow slit between the Strand and the river, and, when I knew it, was dark and comfortless, a blind alley. Gilchrist describes the two rooms on the first floor, front and back, the front room used as a reception-room; a smaller room opened out of it at the back, which was workroom, bedroom, and kitchen in one. The side window looked down through an opening between the houses, showing the river and the hills beyond; and Blake worked at a table facing the window. There seems to be no doubt, from the testimony of many friends, that Crabb Robinson's description, conveys the prejudiced view of a fastidious person, and Palmer, roused by the word 'squalor,' wrote to Gilchrist, asserting 'himself, his wife, and his rooms, were clean and orderly; everything was in its place.' Tatham says that 'he fixed upon these lodgings as being more congenial to his habits, as he was very much accustomed to get out of his bed in the night to write for hours, and return to bed for the rest of the night.' He rarely left the house, except to fetch his pint of porter from the public-house at the corner of the Strand. It was on one of these occasions that he is said to have been cut by a Royal Academician whom he had recently met in society. Had not the Royal Academy been founded (J. T. Smith tells us in his *Book for a Rainy Day*, under date 1768) by 'members who had agreed to withdraw themselves from various clubs, not only in order to be more select as to talent, but perfectly correct as to gentlemanly conduct'?

It was about this time that Blake was discovered, admired, and helped by one who has been described as 'not merely a poet and a painter, an art-critic, an antiquarian, and a writer of prose, an amateur of beautiful things, and a dilettante of things delightful, but also a forger of no mean or ordinary capabilities, and as a subtle and secret poisoner almost without rival in this or any age.' This was Lamb's 'kind, lighthearted Wainewright,' who in the intervals of his strange crimes found time to buy a fine copy of the *Songs of Innocence* and to give a jaunty word of encouragement or advertisement to *Jerusalem*. Palmer remembers Blake stopping before one of Waine-wright's pictures in the Academy and saying, 'Very fine.'

In 1820 Blake had carried out his last commission from Butts in a series of twenty-one drawings in illustration of the Book of Job. In the following year Linnell commissioned from him a duplicate set, and in September 1821 traced them himself from Butts's copies; they were finished, and in parts altered, by Blake. By an agreement dated March 25, 1823, Blake undertook to engrave the designs, which were to be published by Linnell, who gave £100 for the designs and copyright, with the promise of another £100 out of the profits on the sale. There were no profits, but Linnell gave another £50, paying the whole sum of £150 in weekly sums of £2 or £3. The plates are dated March 8, 1825, but they were not published until the date given on the cover, March 1826. Gilchrist intimates that 'much must be lost by the way' in the engraving of the water-colour drawings; but Mr. Russell, a better authority, says that 'marvellous as the original water-colour drawings unquestionably were, they are in every case inferior to the final version in the engraving.' It is on these engravings that the fame of Blake as an artist rests most solidly; invention and execution are here, as he declared that they must always be in great art, equal; imagination at its highest here finds adequate expression, without even the lovely strangeness of a defect. They have been finally praised and defined by Rossetti, in the pages contributed to Gilchrist's life (i. 330—335), of which Mr. Swinburne has said, with little exaggeration, that 'Blake himself, had he undertaken to write notes on his designs, must have done them less justice than this.'

Before Blake had finished engraving the designs to 'Job' he had already begun a new series of illustrations to Dante, also a commission from Linnell; and, with that passionate conscientiousness which was part of the foundation of his genius, he set to work to learn enough Italian to be able to follow the original with the help of Gary's translation. Linnell not only let Blake do the work he wanted to do, paying him for it as he did it, but he took him to see people whom it might be useful for him to know, such as the Aders, who had a house full of books and pictures, and who entertained artists and men of letters. Mrs. Aders had a small amateur talent of her own for painting, and from a letter of Carlyle's, which is preserved among the Crabb Robinson papers, seems to have had literary knowledge as well. 'Has not Mrs. Aders (the lady who lent me *Wilhelm Meister*) great skill in such things?' he asks in a letter full of minute inquiries into German novels. Lamb and Coleridge went to the house, and it was there that Crabb Robinson met Blake in December 1825. Mr. Story, in his Life of Linnell, tells us that one of Linnell's 'most vivid recollections of those days was of hearing Crabb Robinson recite Blake's poem, "The Tiger," before a distinguished company gathered at Mrs. Aders's table. It was a most impressive performance.' We find Blake afterwards at a supper-party at Crabb Robinson's, with Linnell, who notes in his journal going with Blake to Lady Ford's, to see her pictures; in 1820 we find him at Lady Caroline Lamb's.

Along with this general society Blake now gathered about him a certain number of friends and disciples, Linnell being the steadiest friend, and Samuel Palmer, Edward Calvert, and George Richmond the chief disciples. To these must be added, in 1826, Frederick Tatham, a young sculptor, who was to be the betrayer among the disciples. They called Blake's house 'the House of the Interpreter,' and in speaking of it afterwards speak of it always as of holy ground. Thus we hear of Richmond, finding his invention flag, going to seek counsel, and how Blake, who was sitting at tea with his wife, turned to her and said: 'What do we do, Kate, when the visions forsake us?' 'We kneel down and pray, Mr. Blake.' It is Richmond who records a profoundly significant saying of Blake: 'I can look at a knot in a piece of wood till I am frightened at it.' Palmer tells us that Blake and his wife would look into the fire together and draw the figures they saw there, hers quite unlike his, his often terrible. On Palmer's first meeting that Blake, on

October 9, 1824, he tells us that Blake fixed his eyes upon him and said: 'Do you work with fear and trembling?' 'Yes, indeed,' was the reply. 'Then,' said Blake, 'you'll do.'

The friends often met at Hampstead, where Linnell had, in 1824, taken Collins's Farm, at North End, now again known by its old name of 'Wyldes.' Blake disliked the air of Hampstead, which he said always made him ill; but he often went there to see Linnell, and loved the aspect from his cottage, and to sit and hear Mrs. Linnell sing Scotch songs, and would sometimes himself sing his own songs to tunes of his own making. The children loved him, and would watch for him as he came, generally on foot, and one of them says that she remembers 'the cold winter nights when Blake was wrapped up in an old shawl by Mrs. Linnell, and sent on his homeward way, with the servant, lantern in hand, lighting him across the heath to the main road.' It is Palmer's son who reports it, and he adds: 'It is a matter of regret that the record of these meetings and walks and conversations is so imperfect, for in the words of one of Blake's disciples, to walk with him was like "walking with the Prophet Isaiah."' Once when the Palmers were staying at Shoreham, the whole party went down into the country in a carrier's van drawn by eight horses: Calvert tells the story, with picturesque details of Blake's second-sight, and of the hunt with lanterns in Shoreham Castle after a ghost, who turned out to be a snail tapping on the broken glass of the window.

From the end of 1825 Blake's health began to fail, and most of his letters to Linnell contain apologies for not coming to Hampstead, as he is in bed, or is suffering from a cold in the stomach. It was the beginning of that sickness which killed him, described as the mixing of the gall with the blood. He worked persistently, whether he was well or ill, at the Dante drawings, which he made in a folio book given him by Linnell. There were a hundred pages in the book, and he did a drawing on every page, some completely finished, some a mere outline; of these he had only engraved seven at the time of his death. He sat propped up in bed, at work on his drawings, saying, 'Dante goes on the better, which is all I care about.' In a letter to George Cumberland, on April 12, 1827, he writes: 'I have been very near the gates of death, and have returned very weak and an old man, feeble and tottering, but not in the spirit and life, not in the real man, the imagination, which liveth for ever.' And indeed there is no sign of age or weakness in these last great inventions of a dying man.

'Flaxman is gone,' he adds, 'and we must soon follow, every one to his own eternal house, leaving the delusive Goddess Nature to her laws, to get into freedom from all law of the numbers, into the mind, in which every one is king and priest in his own house. God send it so on earth, as it is in heaven.'

Blake died on August 12, 1827, and the ecstasy of his death has been recorded by many witnesses. Tatham tells us how, as he put the finishing touches to a design of 'The Ancient of Days' which he had been colouring for him, he 'threw it down suddenly and said: "Kate, you have been a good wife; I will draw your portrait." She sat near his bed, and he made a drawing which, though not a likeness, is finely touched and expressed. He then threw that down, after having drawn for an hour, and began to sing Hallelujahs and songs of joy and triumph which Mrs. Blake described as being truly sublime in music and in verse.' Smith tells us that he said to his wife, as she stood to hear him, 'My beloved, they are not mine, no, they are not mine.' And a friend quoted by Gilchrist says: 'He died on Sunday night, at six o'clock, in a most glorious manner. He said he was going to that country he had all his life wished to see, and expressed himself happy, hoping for salvation through Jesus Christ. Just before he died his countenance became fair, his eyes brightened, and he burst out into singing of the things he saw in heaven.' 'Perhaps,' he had written not long before, 'and I verily believe it, every death is an improvement of the state of the departed.'

Blake was buried in Bunhill Fields, where all his family had been buried before him, but with the rites of the Church of England, and on August 17 his body was followed to the grave by Calvert, Richmond, Tatham, and Tatham's brother, a clergyman. The burial register reads: 'Aug. 17, 1827. William Blake. Age, 69 years. Brought from Fountain Court, Strand. Grave, 9 feet; E. & W. 77: N. & S. 32. 19/-.' The grave, being a 'common grave,' was used again, and the bones scattered; and this was the world's last indignity against William Blake.

Tatham tells us that, during a marriage of forty-five years, Mrs. Blake had never been separated from her husband 'save for a period that would make altogether about five weeks.' He does not remind us, as Swinburne, on the authority of Seymour Kirkup, reminds us, of Mrs. Blake's one complaint, that her husband was incessantly away 'in Paradise.' Tatham adds: 'After the death of her husband she resided for some time with the author of this, whose domestic arrangements were entirely undertaken by her, until such changes took place that rendered it impossible for her strength to continue in this voluntary office of sincere affection and regard.' Before going to Tatham's she had spent nine months at Linnell's house in Cirencester Place, only leaving it in the summer of 1828, when Linnell let the house. After leaving Tatham she took lodgings in 17 Upper Charlotte Street, Fitzroy Square, where she died at half-past seven on the morning of October 18, 1831, four years after the death of her husband, and within three months of his age. Tatham says: 'Her death not being known but by calculation, sixty-five years were placed upon her coffin,' and in the burial register at Bunhill Fields we read: 'Oct. 23, 1831. Catherine Sophia Blake. Age, 65 yrs. Brought from Upper Charlotte Street, Fitzroy Square.

Grave, 12 feet; E. & W. 7: N. & S. 31, 32. £1, 5s.' She was born April 24, 1762, and was thus aged sixty-nine years and six months.

Swinburne tells us, on the authority of Seymour Kirkup, that, after Blake's death, a gift of £100 was sent to his widow by the Princess Sophia, which she gratefully returned, as not being in actual need of it. Many friends bought copies of Blake's engraved books, some of which Mrs. Blake coloured, with the help of Tatham. After her death all the plates and manuscripts passed into Tatham's hands. In his memoir Tatham says that Blake on his death-bed 'spoke of the writer of this as a likely person to become the manager' of Mrs. Blake's affairs, and he says that Mrs. Blake bequeathed to him 'all of his works that remained unsold at his death, being writings, paintings, and a very great number of copper-plates, of whom impressions may be obtained.' Linnell says that Tatham never showed anything in proof of his assertion that they had been left to him. Tatham had passed through various religious phases, and from being a Baptist, had become an 'angel' of the Irvingite Church. He is supposed to have destroyed the whole of the manuscripts and drawings in his possession on account of religious scruples; and in the life of Calvert by his son we read: 'Edward Calvert, fearing some fatal *dénouement*, went to Tatham and implored him to reconsider the matter and spare the good man's precious work; notwithstanding which, blocks, plates, drawings, and MSS., I understand, were destroyed.'

Such is the received story, but is it strictly true? Did Tatham really destroy these manuscripts for religious reasons, or did he keep them and surreptitiously sell them for reasons of quite another kind? In the *Rossetti Papers* there is a letter from Tatham to Mr. W. M. Rossetti, dated Nov. 6, 1862, in which he says: 'I have sold Mr. Blake's works for thirty years'; and a footnote to Dr. Garnett's monograph on Blake in the *The Portfolio* of 1895 relates a visit from Tatham which took place about 1860. Dr. Garnett told me that Tatham had said, without giving any explanation, that he had destroyed some of Blake's manuscripts and kept others by him, which he had sold from time to time. Is there not therefore a possibility that some of these lost manuscripts may still exist? whether or not they may turn out to be, as Crabb Robinson tells us that Blake told him, 'six or seven epic poems as long as Homer, and twenty tragedies as long as *Macbeth*.'

CHAPTER X

There are people who still ask seriously if Blake was mad. If the mind of Lord Macaulay is the one and only type of sanity, then Blake was mad. If imagination, and ecstasy, and disregard of worldly things, and absorption in the inner world of the mind, and a literal belief in those things which the whole 'Christian community' professes from the tip of its tongue; if these are signs and suspicions of madness, then Blake was certainly mad. His place is where he saw Teresa, among 'the gentle souls who guide the great wine-press of Love'; and, like her, he was 'drunk with intellectual vision.' That drunkenness illuminated him during his whole life, yet without incapacitating him from any needful attention to things by the way. He lived in poverty because he did not need riches; but he died without leaving a debt. He was a steady, not a fitful worker, and his wife said of him that she never saw his hands still unless he was reading or asleep. He was gentle and sudden; his whole nature was in a steady heat which could blaze at any moment into a flame. 'A saint amongst the infidels and a heretic with the orthodox,' he has been described by one who knew him best in his later years, John Linnell; and Palmer has said of him: 'His love of art was so great that he would see nothing but art in anything he loved; and so, as he loved the Apostles and their divine Head (for so I believe he did), he must needs say that they were all artists.' 'When opposed by the superstitious, the crafty, or the proud,' says Linnell again, 'he outraged all common-sense and rationality by the opinions he advanced'; and Palmer gives an instance of it: 'Being irritated by the exclusively scientific talk at a friend's house, which talk had turned on the vastness of space, he cried out, "It is false. I walked the other evening to the end of the heath, and touched the sky with my finger."'

It was of the essence of Blake's sanity that he could always touch the sky with his finger. 'To justify the soul's frequent joy in what cannot be defined to the intellectual part, or to calculation': that, which is Walt Whitman's definition of his own aim, defines

Blake's. Where others doubted he knew; and he saw where others looked vaguely into the darkness. He saw so much further than others into what we call reality, that others doubted his report, not being able to check it for themselves; and when he saw truth naked he did not turn aside his eyes. Nor had he the common notion of what truth is, or why it is to be regarded. He said: 'When I tell a truth it is not for the sake of convincing those who do not know it, but for the sake of defending those who do.' And his criterion of truth was the inward certainty of instinct or intuition, not the outward certainty of fact. 'God forbid,' he said, 'that Truth should be confined to mathematical demonstration. He who does not know Truth at sight is unworthy of her notice.' And he said: 'Error is created, truth is eternal. Error or creation will be burned up, and then, not till then, truth or eternity will appear. It is burned up the moment men cease to behold it.'

It was this private certainty in regard to truth and all things that Blake shared with the greatest minds of the world, and men doubted him partly because he was content to possess that certainty and had no desire to use it for any practical purpose, least of all to convince others. He asked to be believed when he spoke, told the truth, and was not concerned with argument or experiment, which seemed to him ways of evasion. He said:

It is easy to acknowledge a man to be great and good, while we
Derogate from him in the trifles and small articles of that goodness,
Those alone are his friends who admire his minutest powers.'

He spoke naturally in terms of wisdom, and made no explanations, bridged none of the gulfs which it seemed to him so easy to fly over. Thus when he said that Ossian and Rowley were authentic, and that what Macpherson and Chatterton said was ancient was so, he did not mean it in a strictly literal sense, but in the sense in which ancient meant authentic: true to ancient truth. Is a thing true as poetry? then it is true in the minutest because the most essential sense. On the other hand, in saying that part of Wordsworth's Preface was written by another hand, he was merely expressing in a bold figure a sane critical opinion. Is a thing false among many true things? then it is not the true man who is writing it, but some false section of his brain. It may be dangerous practically to judge all things at an inner tribunal; but it is only by such judgments that truth moves.

And truth has moved, or we have. After *Zarathustra, Jerusalem* no longer seems a wild heresy. People were frightened because they were told that Blake was mad, or a blasphemer. Nietzsche, who has cleared away so many obstructions from thought, has shamed us from hiding behind these treacherous and unavailing defences. We have come to realise, what Rossetti pointed out long ago, that, as a poet, Blake's characteristic is above all things that of 'pure perfection in *writing verse*.' We no longer praise his painting for its qualities as literature, or forget that his design has greatness as design. And of that unique creation of an art out of the mingling of many arts which we see in the 'illuminated printing' of the engraved books, we have come to realise what Palmer meant when he said long ago: 'As a picture has been said to be something between a thing and a thought, so, in some of these type books over which Blake had long brooded with his brooding of fire, the very paper seems to come to life as you gaze upon it—not with a mortal life, but an indestructible life.' And we have come to realise what Blake meant by the humble and arrogant things which he said about himself. 'I doubt not yet,' he writes in one of those gaieties of speech which illuminate his letters, 'to make a figure in the great dance of life that shall amuse the spectators in the sky.' If there are indeed spectators there, amused by our motions, what dancer among us are they more likely to have approved than this joyous, untired, and undistracted dancer to the eternal rhythm?